It was her face—her face on the body of a stranger. Even in the fuzzy photo, the likeness was unmistakable: the same slightly slanted eyes, high cheekbones, and pointy chin, the long straight blonde hair, even the nose with the tiny bump on it that she hated.

Who was this girl in the old picture, gazing out at Emma with the same scowl that had just crossed her own face? Emma jumped to her feet, bending forward to see the screen more clearly.

"It's you, Emma!" Revi shrieked, throwing her arms into the air. "I swear, it's you."

"It can't be. This picture was taken almost twenty years ago," Emma protested. "It's just a coincidence, that's all." But she felt a coldness in the pit of her stomach, seeing her face there on the nameless young woman . . .

SHADOW SELF

Cheryl Zach

BERKLEY JAM BOOKS, NEW YORK

SHADOW SELF

A Berkley Jam Book / published by arrangement with
the author

PRINTING HISTORY
Berkley Jam edition / December 2000

All rights reserved.
Copyright © 2000 by Cheryl Zach.
This book, or parts thereof, may not be reproduced in any form
without permission.
For information address: The Berkley Publishing Group,
a division of Penguin Putnam Inc.,
375 Hudson Street, New York, New York 10014.

The Penguin Putnam Inc. World Wide Web site address is
http://www.penguinputnam.com

ISBN: 0-425-17772-6

BERKLEY JAM BOOKS®
Berkley Jam Books are published by The Berkley Publishing Group,
a division of Penguin Putnam Inc.,
375 Hudson Street, New York, New York 10014.
BERKLEY JAM and its logo
are trademarks belonging to Penguin Putnam Inc.

PRINTED IN THE UNITED STATES OF AMERICA

10 9 8 7 6 5 4 3 2 1

For Stephanie and Judy,
friends through sunshine and shadow

Prologue

Dear Diary:

I dreamed again last night. I felt the horror, the pain, just as if it were happening for the first time. I was there on the sidewalk, with the rest of our group clustered in a loose circle. Around me, I could hear the mob—people yelling, shouting ugly names—and I staggered from the rough, shoving hands. I was being thrust away from my friends— I tried to find a familiar face, reached for a hand that I trusted, but it wasn't there.

Low and deep beneath the shouts of the crowd, I heard the K-9 dogs growl, their lips drawn back over fangs that I could already feel tearing my skin. I saw the blue uniforms, the closed faces as the police moved to push us back. Then I looked around, searching for the one face most important to me, so we could blend into the rest of the mob and slip away.

But he didn't come. I stumbled through the crowd, trying to find him, glancing into the nearest building . . .

Then fire blossomed behind the glass door, and splin-

ters of glass exploded outward, with a wave of sound that knocked me to my knees.

I felt the fear in my throat and the wetness of blood trickling down my face, and I knew something had gone terribly wrong . . .

Chapter
One

On the afternoon that would change her life forever, Emma Carter sat in her father's study with her best friend, both peering at the computer screen. Fidgeting with impatience, Emma chewed on one fingernail. Afterward, she would remember only how ordinary the day had been, with no hint of the shattering revelations to come.

"Are we done yet?" Emma demanded. "I've got a date, remember?"

"Look at those clothes—what a joke!" Revi Feldman ran one hand through her auburn curls and leaned closer to the computer screen. "Emma, you're not looking."

Emma glanced at her watch, instead. "How much longer is this going to take? Ms. Patterson gives too many of these flipping reports."

"We're almost done," her best friend said, her tone soothing. "This is the best on-line encyclopedia we've checked yet. We just need to print out a couple more of these articles to show that we did our research."

If they didn't have the most demanding social studies

teacher at Oak Grove High, this wouldn't be necessary, Emma thought, scowling. "Jay was going to pick me up ten minutes ago," she reminded her friend. "I need to change clothes and go watch for his car."

"So, you know Jay's always late. Just because he's the best-looking senior at Oak Grove . . ." Revi giggled and glanced toward Emma. "And the best kisser?"

"Wouldn't you like to know," Emma joked back, but her bad mood was slipping away. "He thinks he's worth waiting for, I guess." Soon, she'd be speeding along in Jay's red convertible and she could forget about boring history reports.

Then she felt Revi stiffen. "Oh, migod, Emma. That's you!"

Emma turned back to the computer screen; they had been viewing an article on protest groups over the last fifty years. To collect information for their report, they had read about all types of oddball groups, from the Refusal to Recognize Liberated Women to the more widespread civil rights, gay rights, women's rights, and animal rights organizations. But this did not prepare Emma for the faded black-and-white photo that she saw, a little blurred on the computer screen.

It was her face—her face on the body of a stranger. Even in the fuzzy photo, the likeness was unmistakable: the same slightly slanted eyes, high cheekbones, and pointy chin, the long straight blonde hair, even the nose with the tiny bump on it that she hated.

Who was this girl in the old picture, gazing out at Emma with the same scowl that had just crossed her own face? Emma jumped to her feet, bending forward to see the screen more clearly.

"It's you, Emma!" Revi shrieked, throwing her arms into the air. "I swear, it's you."

"It can't be. This picture was taken almost twenty years ago," Emma protested. "It's just a coincidence, that's all." But she felt a coldness in the pit of her stomach, seeing her face there on the nameless young woman who stood among a crowd of protestors; they all carried homemade signs and wore T-shirts with environmental slogans.

"Coincidence? No way. Maybe it's your clone. Or—"

"You've been watching too many episodes of *The X-Files*!" Emma snapped. "Get your mind out of fantasy land, for heaven's sakes."

The sound of a car horn cut through her increasingly agitated thoughts. "There's Jay, and I'm not even ready. You finish printing out the report research, please. I've got to change clothes."

"But what about this photo?" Revi demanded.

"Forget it!" Emma almost shouted. "It's a freak accident, that's all. Lots of people look the same."

"Not like this," Revi repeated stubbornly.

Emma frowned at her friend. "I said, forget it." Turning her back on the computer desk and Revi's inquisitive, too-bright brown eyes, Emma stormed out of the room, up the stairs to her bedroom and into her walk-in closet, where she hastily pulled clothes off their hangers. Jay was an incredible catch, and she didn't want to try his patience too long. He might be late, but he didn't expect her to be. It was one of his weaknesses, true, but his incredible good looks and smooth charm more than made up for a few drawbacks. You couldn't have everything. He was smart and funny and he liked her; they had fun together.

Pulling her T-shirt off and peeling out of her jeans, Emma shrugged into her new blue sweater and tugged the matching short skirt up over her hips. She ran a comb through her long blonde hair and glanced into the mirror on the back of the closet door.

Blue-green eyes set at a slight slant, high cheekbones, pointed chin, nose with that annoying bump in its bridge. She'd been trying to get her physician dad to agree to plastic surgery since she'd been ten, but he was holding out for eighteen—six more months to go. It wasn't all that common a face—how could a stranger look so similar?

No, she refused to think about it now. She hurried out of the closet and ran for the stairwell. When she reached the ground floor, she called to Revi, "See you later and thanks for finishing without me."

"Yeah, right," Revi answered, but her tone was good-natured. "Call me later, okay?"

"Sure. Lock the door when you leave."

They had been alone in the sprawling colonial-style house. It was Thursday. Emma knew that her mother was still at the homeless shelter where she volunteered three afternoons a week; her brothers had walked over to the park where their ball game would be held in an hour or so, and her dad would still be at the hospital, of course. As she headed for the door, a curly mass of brown-and-white sprang up from the throw rug and launched itself at her knees.

"Down, Happy, down," she directed the elderly cocker spaniel, who yipped with the contagious glee that had earned the dog his name. She stopped long enough to rub his ears, then heard another honk from the driveway. "I'm late; I'll see you later."

Happy whined, but retreated to his favorite spot at the side of the hall where he could keep up with the comings and goings of all the family members.

Emma grabbed her purse from the hall table and opened the door. The air outside was balmy with a Midwestern spring, the sunshine bright, and the sky blue. A perfect day for a ride in a convertible, Emma thought, her spirits lifting. She waved at Jay, who sat with one arm sprawled across the back of the bucket seats.

"About time," he called, his tone teasing. "Get in."

She opened the passenger door of the low-slung sports car and slid into the seat, leaning over to give Jay a quick kiss. He smelt of the latest male cologne, and his knit shirt wore a designer name over the pocket. He could have been a model, Emma thought, not for the first time. His sleek blond hair, his pale blue eyes, wide smile and enviably well-shaped nose made him the best-looking boy at school. Add to that his tall frame and broad shoulders, and she knew that half the female population envied her status as Jay's girlfriend.

Not that Emma was unpopular herself, but still—Jay was a catch, no doubt about it. He kissed her once more, then straightened.

"Where would you like to go?"

"It's a beautiful day." She leaned back in the leather seat and watched the faint line of wispy clouds that edged the deep blue of the sky. "We could drive to the lake."

"Too far, and the traffic will be too heavy," Jay objected, pulling out of the drive.

"Ride out into the country?"

"To do what—ogle the cornfields?" Jay asked, practical as always.

Emma stifled a sigh and pushed a blonde strand out of her eyes as the car accelerated and the wind whipped her hair. "So, what do you want to do?"

"Ride out to the mall; there's a new video game out today I wanted to check out."

"Sure," Emma said. She leaned back in her seat, turning away from him as she clicked her seat belt into place. Just what they always did, she thought. But still, it was with Jay, and that was the point, right?

She enjoyed the brief drive, and when Jay maneuvered the sports car into a slot in the parking lot, she walked beside him into the mall. The shopping mall was crowded with after-school teens, mothers with small babies in tow, and older couples walking side by side.

Sweet, she thought, glancing at one gray-haired couple, if a little boring, like her own parents: undemonstrative but quietly fond of each other. Her father worked long hours at the hospital, and her mother volunteered her time at numerous charities, but they both were always ready to stop and support their children's activities. Her mom would get home in time to go and see her brothers play ball this evening, and her dad would hurry in at the last minute, climbing the park bleachers to the spot her mom would be saving. They would share a large bag of popcorn and cheer loudly. Emma smiled a little as she pictured it, remembering her own softball years, when her younger brothers were still too small to join a team.

Jay was already absorbed in the newest version of his favorite computer game. Bored, Emma scanned the shelves. Here was a makeover disk that looked interesting. Emma read the print on the back of the video box, wondering if this would show her how she would look after a nose job removed that offensive bump on the bridge of her nose. She wished she could convince her dad to let her have the surgery this summer instead of next year. Then she glanced at the shelf above and saw a photo kit. Scan your favorite snapshots into the computer, the banner read. Crop and reduce, blow up your photos. Add your face onto famous people's bodies . . .

With a tightening in her stomach, she remembered the photo she and Revi had seen on the research disk. For a moment, she wondered idly if someone had played a vicious joke. But surely a reputable encyclopedia company wouldn't allow people to play around with their old photos.

Could Revi have pulled a prank? No, that was stupid. Emma chewed on one fingernail, thinking about it. Not only was the on-line encyclopedia protected against tampering, Revi didn't have the computer skills to pull it off. The resemblance in the photo was only a stupid coincidence, just as Emma had said. It wasn't worth thinking about. So why did it keep popping up in her mind, pulling her out of a pleasant few hours of escape with her boyfriend?

Sighing, Emma pushed her troublesome thoughts aside and walked back to Jay's side. "Find what you wanted?" she asked.

"Yeah," Jay said. "Look at these graphics—this will be so much more advanced that the version I've got now."

"Fun," Emma agreed, though she thought the picture on the carton, with its dripping blood, looked entirely too realistic for her taste.

Jay paid for the computer game, then they wandered down to the food court and ordered frozen yogurt. When their order came, they sat down at one of the little metal tables and ate their snack. In the background, rock music played, and a baby in a stroller wailed and rubbed its eyes.

"Can you believe school will be out in another two weeks?" Emma said. "No more reports, no more exams—" She rolled her eyes at the thought.

"When do you and Revi leave for Florida?" Jay dipped his spoon into his yogurt.

"Two weeks after school is out." She took a bite of the light, sweet, peach-flavored dessert.

"Gone for a whole month, huh? What am I going to do without you?"

Emma wasn't sure she wanted to consider that; too many girls coveted Jay's attention. "That's the question, isn't it?" she said, her tone a little dry.

Jay flashed his wide smile. "Aha, jealous, are we? I love it." He leaned closer, his chair wobbling a little, and gave her a quick kiss, his lips cold from the frozen dessert.

An older woman in the next booth sniffed in disapproval, and a little girl with cookie crumbs on her chin watched wide-eyed. Despite the audience, Emma allowed the kiss to linger, just for a moment, then reluctantly drew back. "You better not forget me while I'm communing with the dolphins."

The private school that she, Revi, Jay and her other friends attended always offered a wide variety of summer programs. She and Revi had debated the classes available, then applied for intern positions at a dolphin research institute. It would take them from their prosperous Chicago suburb to the Florida coast, with a beach to play on in their off-duty hours. Emma's parents had agreed it would be an educational experience, and best of all, it sounded like fun.

Jay winked. "As if I could forget my favorite girl," he told her. "My volunteer post last summer at the United Nations was great, and New York was a blast. But this year, with Yale coming up in the fall, I want to take some high-level language courses and brush up on my math, so I'll be ready for the Ivy League."

Emma nodded. Jay had secret ambitions toward a political career, and his smooth good looks and articulate charm, not to mention his father's money, made his goals seem reasonable. She could picture him as a senator, someday, leaning back with the same casual charm that he projected now sitting in an off-balance metal chair and licking yogurt off his fingers.

She took a bite of her crunchy cone and tried not to think about Jay going off to college. At least they still had a lot of the summer to share, despite Emma's trip.

When they finished eating, they wandered through the mall, holding hands. When Jay paused to look in the window of a sports store, Emma gazed at the glass, too, but instead of seeing the ski display, she stared at her own reflection instead.

Pale and ghostly, the face and the form were familiar, yet now they seemed alien, strange. It reminded her too vividly of the old photo in the on-line article. If this were a movie, there'd be creepy music right now, Emma thought sourly. But the whole thing was weird, and she found the strange picture harder to forget that she had imagined.

Who was the girl in the photo, the one who had gazed at the newsman's camera almost twenty years ago? Why did she share Emma's face, her eyes, her frown?

And why couldn't Emma forget her?

Chapter
Two

When they left the mall, Jay dropped Emma at her house. "See you tomorrow," he called.

Emma nodded and waved. When she went inside, the chubby little cocker spaniel rushed up, barking happily, but otherwise, the house was empty. She felt a stab of guilt for missing her brothers' game, but, hey, there would be plenty more.

She climbed the stairs to her room and changed her clothes, putting her jeans and T-shirt back on. When she heard the metallic shriek of the garage door opening, she thought, Game over, and went downstairs to greet the returning athletes.

Her youngest brother, Ethan, came in first, his baseball glove in one hand, his cap still pulled down over his sweat-damp blond hair. "We lost," the ten-year-old said, his tone bleak as he leaned over to rub the dog's head. The animal's short tail wagged briskly as it sniffed Ethan's trousers.

Emma patted his shoulder; his shirt was stained with dust and perspiration. "Too bad, Ethan. Did you get to play?"

"Two innings," he said. "I caught a fly ball! How come you weren't there?"

"Good for you," Emma said. "I—uh—I had a report to finish for school." She pushed aside the memory of her afternoon date with Jay. "I'll come to the next game," she promised.

Her other brother came through the door. Taller and skinnier than Ethan, twelve-year-old Todd had a backpack thrown across one shoulder and his baseball glove in one hand. "Won't be any more games," he said. "We lost, so we don't play again."

"Oh," Emma said. "I'm sorry."

Todd scowled. "I struck out in the last inning."

"Bad luck," she commiserated. "You'll do better next time."

"No, I suck," Todd said glumly. "Don't know why I even bother to play."

"Don't be so hard on yourself, sweetheart." Their mother shut the door behind her. "You're a good shortstop, and that's one of the hardest positions to play, Dad says."

"Where is Dad?" Emma asked.

"Right behind us. He drove straight from the hospital," her mother said, pushing back a strand of graying hair. "So he's in the Jeep. After the game, we stopped at the vegetarian deli for a sandwich; have you eaten?"

Emma nodded, hoping her mom wouldn't ask for details. Her mother was big on healthy eating; she probably wouldn't think much of frozen yogurt as a choice for dinner.

"Boys, better get onto your homework; it's getting late." Her mother glanced at them. "And you need a bath before bed."

"I'm too tired," Ethan complained, slumping down onto one of the chairs that surrounded the table in the breakfast nook. "Emma, will you help me with my math, please?"

"Emm-ma, help me ple-ase," Todd mimicked, making a face at his younger brother. "Don't be such a baby."

"I said please!" Ethan responded, his tone indignant. "And you ask Emma for help all the time."

Todd frowned. "Do not."

"Do, too!"

Todd aimed a quick jab at his brother, but Emma stepped between them and deflected the blow. "Behave yourself, brat," she told her middle sibling.

Todd stuck out his tongue. Emma moved quickly, her hand darting toward his mouth, as if to grab it. He jumped back hastily, and their mother, who had been glancing through the stack of mail she had brought in, rubbed absently at the old burn scars on the side of her face.

"Get a move on, boys," she said.

"Emma?" Ethan asked, his tone hopeful.

"Oh, all right," Emma said with a dramatic sigh. "But I have an English essay to write, so it better not take too long."

The boys were climbing the staircase when their father walked in through the garage door. Emma paused for his quick hug; the antiseptic scent of the hospital still clung to him, and his brown eyes were tired. He had the knack of making patients feel at ease, safe; she could see why her mom had fallen in love with him when he was only a struggling young medical student.

"Hi, Dad," she said. "Long day?"

"Yes, I had my first surgery at seven this morning," he admitted. "I'm ready for a cup of tea and my easychair."

She grinned at him, and Todd hung over the banister to interrupt. "Dad, will you help me with my science homework?"

Their father rolled his eyes. "How about Emma—"

"She's helping Ethan," Todd explained. "It won't take long, honest. And Mom's no good in science, she says so herself."

"All right, I'll be right up," their dad agreed. "Let me take off my jacket."

"Ha," Ethan called from his bedroom. "Who's a baby now?"

Todd ran up the last of the steps and disappeared into the bedroom; she heard a muffled exclamation, then Ethan called, "I'm telling! Mom!"

"Crybaby," Todd jeered.

Emma climbed the steps, shaking her head. Her brothers were a pain, sometimes. She thought of the coming weeks in Florida, with no one but Revi to share her dorm room with, and lots of free time on the beach. Life was good.

But when Ethan's homework was done and she went downstairs to the study to write the rough draft of her essay, she found the printouts that Revi had done sitting on the desk. And there was the photo—Revi had printed it, too, without even asking.

Emma stared at the black-and-white photo for a moment, then turned it facedown against the pile of papers. She didn't want any more reminders of the mystery girl.

"Just forget it," she muttered to herself as she clicked on the word-processing software. "Forget it, it's a stupid coincidence, that's all."

But later, when she climbed the steps and got into bed, she shut her eyes and the image returned, pale and ghostly, to haunt her thoughts. It took a long time to fall asleep, and when she did, her dreams were troubled, though she didn't quite remember them when she woke Thursday morning.

She just knew she felt tired still, and irritable. When she came downstairs, her brothers had already eaten, and the table was littered with bits of cereal and sticky with spilled sugar. Emma toasted an English muffin and ate it standing at the breakfast table, sipping orange juice and trying to push aside the strange pall of depression that hung over her.

This was stupid. School was almost out; she had a great summer planned. Why worry over such a trivial thing?

But when she packed her articles and her finished essay into her backpack, she saw the photo again and frowned. She picked up the printout, ready to tear it into pieces, but something held her back. She thrust it into the bottom of her backpack instead, and hurried out to the garage.

She was almost late to school, and she had to run to make it to her first class. She didn't have time to talk to Revi until lunch, and it didn't help when her best friend came in carrying a library book that she held up before Emma's face.

"I have just the thing for you!" Revi cried. "See, you need to read this. It's all about reincarnation."

"What?" Emma took a bite of her taco; the shell cracked and she leaned over her plate, trying not to lose all of the cheese, lettuce, and tomato.

"Reincarnation. You know, how you can be reborn in someone else's body."

"This is for another report?" Emma asked, keeping her tone steady with an effort.

"No, silly, this is about that photograph—the mystery girl with your face!" The clatter in the cafeteria seemed even louder than usual, and Revi raised her voice slightly.

"Revi, I am not reincarnated!" Emma snapped. "And don't tell the whole world your dumb theories. Why are you so hung up on that stupid picture?"

"Stupid? I think it's fascinating. And how do you know you're not living another life? I mean, if that girl—who-ever she was—had died a year or two after that photo— some tragic accident, maybe—you could have been born the same year, a new body with her spirit."

"I am not—" Emma wanted to shake her friend; she glared at Revi, who shrugged.

"Okay, okay, don't yell. It's just one theory."

"I suppose you have more?" Emma stabbed a fork so hard into her salad that half the lettuce slipped off her plate. "I don't want to hear them, thank you so much."

"Geez, what side of the bed did you get up on?" Revi sounded hurt. "I'm just trying to help. If it were me, I'd want to know."

The problem was, she did, Emma thought. She did want to know.

The two girls put up their trays and walked down to the restroom, and Emma ducked into a stall. When she came out, she washed her hands, trying not to look into the mirror on the wall. Staring at her own reflection only reminded her of the pale image of the news photo. Same face, same hair, same bumpy nose . . .

She couldn't even look at herself in the mirror anymore. Could Revi possibly be right? Did Emma have a connection with the stranger in the photo—something weird . . . a psychic link?

No, she was getting as strange as Revi, Emma told herself, turning abruptly away from the sink. No way.

She wouldn't think about it anymore, and of course, she could think of nothing else. In her next class, the chemistry teacher droned on unheard, while Emma fought the usual after-lunch dullness. Every time she looked into the smooth surface of the lab table, she saw a ghostly half-image of a thin face and long light-colored hair.

How could she lay this ghost to rest? Emma wondered. How long would this picture haunt her? Would she ever know the answer to the puzzle?

Jay met her in the hall before their last class, throwing one arm casually around her shoulders. "I can't come over to your house this afternoon," he told her. "I have a meeting with the grad dance committee. Sorry."

Emma nodded. "That's okay," she said automatically. "I have something I need to work on, anyhow." It seemed like a sign. When he turned off for his own class, Emma paused in the hallway long enough to pull the wrinkled print from the bottom of her backpack. She looked again at the girl in the photo. There might be more pictures somewhere, even a name.

She drove home quickly and left her little car in the driveway. In the kitchen, she found their part-time house-keeper, Sandy, humming to herself as she mopped the tile floor.

"Want anything from the fridge?" the middle-aged woman called cheerfully. "Speak now, or you don't get nothing till the floor dries."

"I'm okay, thanks anyhow," Emma answered. "I've got some work to do."

She walked on into her dad's study and was annoyed to find her brothers hanging over the desk, focused on the computer screen. Happy lay curled up at their feet, and the dog raised its head and barked when she walked into the room.

"What are you, the early warning system?" Emma quipped, leaning over to pet the spaniel, whose tail wagged briskly.

Todd had pushed a key quickly, but not before she got a glance of a brightly colored image of half-clothed women.

"Off," she ordered. "You know Dad doesn't want you using this computer. You're too young to be searching the 'net for smut. Anyhow, I have school work to do."

Ethan flushed and looked away, but his brother was made of tougher stuff.

"I wasn't," Todd said, his voice innocent. "We were just looking for a good computer game. And I don't want to use the other computer; it's not as fast."

"It's also got a child guard on it," Emma pointed out dryly. "To keep you out of sites like that. But it's fine for your games. Go."

Todd stood up reluctantly, but he fired one parting shot before he headed for the door. "And I suppose you're doing research again."

"Not being interested in naked strangers, yes, that's

what I'm doing," Emma answered, her tone dignified. But as soon as her brothers were out of sight, the cocker spaniel pattering along behind them, she slipped into the chair, ready to search the newspaper archives for anything that might give her more information about the mystery teen she and Revi had discovered, the girl with Emma's face.

While the search engine came into view, Emma pulled the print of the photo from her backpack and looked at the caption. There were no names of the people in the picture, but it did tell the location: Los Angeles.

She first tried the *Los Angeles Times*, but when she went to the Archives section, she found that the on-line archives only went back to 1985. She frowned; this was probably not early enough for her purposes, but just to be sure she scanned the '85 and '86 issues. Here she was frustrated again; the archives had only the text of the paper, not the photos, and Emma had no name to attach to the mystery girl.

She exited the program and pushed herself away from the keyboard. She would have to try something else. There wasn't enough in the on-line newspaper files for her to check; where else could she find clues to the stranger's identity?

The library, of course; she might find more information there. She found Sandy sitting on a dining room chair, drinking a cup of tea. "I'm going to the library, Sandy. Tell Mom when she comes in, okay?"

"Sure thing." The housekeeper raised one pale brow. "Don't study too hard."

Emma grinned and grabbed her car keys from the table by the door. When she reached the local branch library, Emma parked her car and folded the photo printout, tucking it into her jeans' pocket. Inside, she waited at the research librarian's desk while an older woman nattered on about growing roses and finding the right soil conditions. When Emma's time came, she explained briefly what she needed, and the librarian led her to a microfiche machine. After they had located all the available newspaper files from the early eighties, Emma sat down in the plastic chair.

This library only held *Chicago Tribune* back issues, so unless the mystery's girl's activities had gained nationwide attention, Emma was doomed to failure. But she had to try.

It was slow work, scanning articles from issue after issue, especially since Emma didn't really know what she was looking for. Emma felt very isolated in the back room where the microfiche was stored, and the fading sunlight outside the one narrow window only added to her feelings of loneliness.

The hum of the machine was the only sound she could hear, and the room smelled dusty and empty. Still, she had the feeling that someone was watching her, but when Emma glanced over her shoulder, she saw no one.

She was being stupid, Emma told herself crossly. She had listened too often to Revi's conspiracy theories. Yet Emma could not help feeling another presence here—a pale image with Emma's long fair hair and pointed face— trying to gaze over her shoulder, trying to tell her something . . .

Stupid, stupid. It was only her imagination, Emma told herself for the tenth time, only her own nervous qualms. But even so, she felt as if a face from the past peered over her shoulder, and a voiceless cry echoed in the silence, trying to warn her about dangerous secrets . . .

When the lights flickered, signaling the warning for closing time, Emma had found nothing. Her head ached and her eyes were tired from squinting at the hard-to-read letters on the screen. Maybe there was nothing to find, she told herself. She was on a wild-goose chase, almost certainly. The girl in the picture must be no one important, and Emma was acting totally nuts.

But when she stood, Emma glanced again over her shoulder. The fluorescent neon lights allowed no real shadows in the library room, yet regardless, she felt as if a shadow dogged her steps. Emma had to know the truth. She had to find out more.

When she headed for the exit, she paused at the research librarian's desk. "Is there anywhere I could find other newspapers from the early eighties?"

The woman nodded. "Of course. You can go into the city and check one of the larger libraries. I'm sure they will have more back issues available." She glanced at her watch.

Emma took the hint. "Thanks." She walked slowly to her car, thinking hard. She didn't want to drive into Chicago alone; the traffic was horrendous, even if she went over the weekend. Emma drove home in the falling dusk, telling herself again that she should forget the whole thing.

At home, Sandy had departed, and Emma's mom was stirring a pot of her special spaghetti sauce on the stove. Her brothers tossed a foam ball back and forth in the hallway, while Happy barked furiously and ran from one to the other.

Todd flashed his sister a beseeching look when Emma walked into the house. She made a face at him, but when she hugged her mom, she didn't mention the boys' forbidden foray into 'net porn.

"How was school?" her mother asked, kissing her cheek before returning to the simmering sauce. "Find what you needed at the library?"

"Okay, and no, I think I need to go to a bigger library," Emma explained. "Umm, that smells good."

"What are you looking for?" her mother asked, putting down her spoon to drop noodles into a pot of boiling water.

Emma was tempted to tell her mother everything, but just then the boys burst into the kitchen, still tossing the ball, and her mother turned her head.

"Todd, careful with that! You two go wash your hands."

Emma changed her mind. "Just some history research," she said vaguely. "Want me to make a salad?"

"Yes, please," her mother said. "Happy, sit down."

The dog retreated to its usual spot on the mat beside the door, and Emma began to wash lettuce and tomatoes and broccoli, and the moment passed.

After dinner, she went up to her bedroom and called Revi.

"What's up?" her friend said, her voice slurred as if she had her mouth full.

"Are you eating dinner? Sorry," Emma said.

"Just finishing a pear," Revi told her. "Did you figure out that math page?"

"Yeah, I'll tell you in a minute," Emma said. "Listen, can you drive into Chicago with me on Saturday?"

"I guess. What for? Shopping?" Revi sounded hopeful. "Can we go to Nordstrom's, or downtown to Marshall Fields?"

"Maybe, but I want to hit a library first," Emma said, hoping her friend would say yes. Somehow, she didn't want to be alone in a library again, with the whispery non-sound of a voice from the past echoing in her ears.

"What for? We finished our report; it's on Ms. Patterson's desk," Revi said.

"I know, but I want to—to look for more photos of that girl we saw in the encyclopedia article."

"Oh wow," Revi breathed. "You bet I'll come."

They talked a few minutes about the math homework, then Emma hung up the phone. She looked once more at the creased and much folded printout, trying to see into the other girl's eyes, search her mind across time and space.

"Who are you?" Emma muttered. "And why are you haunting me?"

Chapter
Three

All day Friday Emma thought about the coming library search. She could hardly listen in class, and she was still distracted Friday night when she went out with Jay.

"What's up with you, Em?" her boyfriend demanded. "Don't you want to hear what I'm telling you?"

"Sure." Emma hastily pulled her thoughts back to her date.

"So, what did I say?" Jay frowned.

"Umm, you were talking about the classes you're taking," Emma guessed, hoping she was right.

Jay nodded, relaxing. "Yeah, well, I think the Latin class will be a help when I get into college. You should take Latin next year, Em, and another math class. They look for these things on your college admissions."

"Good idea," Emma agreed. But as soon as he'd slipped back into an absorbed monologue, her thoughts wandered again. Everywhere she went, the girl from the past followed like a shadow that even brightest sunlight could not erase. The more Emma tried to put her out of her mind, the more the intruder resurfaced.

For once it was a relief when Jay took her home. He kissed her hard before they got out of the convertible, running his hand up her torso to cup her breast. "My girl," he breathed, bending over to kiss her neck.

Usually, she would have responded, but tonight, even Jay's practiced kisses couldn't drag her thoughts back from the abstraction she had been lost in all day. She felt sluggish, not quite there, and his touch was almost irritating.

She pulled away, and when he looked at her in surprise, she leaned closer to kiss him lightly. "I'd better go in," she said. "Last weekend, my dad wanted to know just what we found to talk about so long in the driveway."

Jay made a face. "We could go to my house," he suggested. "I think my parents are still out."

She shook her head. "Not tonight. I'd better go in," she repeated.

Jay grimaced, but he leaned back against the seat. "I guess. You know I'm busy tomorrow and most of Sunday with that community service project at the nursing home."

Emma nodded. "That's great of you to spend your weekend painting and cleaning," she said.

"Yeah, community service looks good on my resumé," he agreed.

Emma stifled a sigh. At least he was honest, she told herself. She kissed him again, then went inside.

In the hall, Happy came to sniff her and accept his usual pat on the head. Her dad looked out of the study. "Hi, Emma," he greeted. "Have a good time?"

She nodded, glad there had been no heavy making out tonight, glad she could meet his eyes easily. "The movie was good," she said. "Then we went for pizza."

Her dad came closer and ruffled her hair, as if she were a little girl again. Emma leaned against his shoulder for a moment, wondering if she could explain about the picture from the past that haunted her.

But the phone rang in the study, and her father looked back over his shoulder.

"Expecting a call?" she asked.

"I was hoping not," he said soberly. "We had a dicey triple bypass today; I worried about complications." He headed for the study to answer.

Emma sighed. But she had come to terms with her father's demanding schedule long ago; he saved people's lives, and if that meant he wasn't always there for his children's every whim, they had to accept it. She knew he cared about his family—but when his patients needed him, that need had to be answered.

Left alone, Emma turned for the stairs. Tomorrow, she told herself, tomorrow she would find some answers, she just knew it.

Revi was bubbling with excitement when Emma picked her up Saturday morning. "It reminds me of the trips my mom and I used to take into the city," she explained. "Since my grandmother's been sick, Mom never has time to go anymore."

Emma nodded, her attention on the road. The multiple lanes of traffic zoomed along until they approached the downtown area, then a stalled tanker truck slowed the lines of cars and trucks to a crawl. At last, they reached their exit and spent the next thirty minutes locating a place to park. Then they locked the car doors and walked three blocks to Revi's favorite department store.

Inside Marshall Fields, they paused briefly to look through a display of handbags, then took the escalators up, up to the Walnut Room. When they were escorted into the cavernous restaurant and shown to a table, Emma glanced around at the heavy dark wood that framed the room and ran her fingers over the smooth linen that clothed the table.

A few feet away, a pianist in a dinner jacket played a grand piano, his fingers stroking the ivory and black keys with practiced ease. The classical music rose and fell in calming waves of melody, cloaking the clatter of silverware and the clink of glasses, and at the next table, three blue-rinsed grandmotherly types chatted about a vacation in France.

"Very uptown," she told Revi, grinning.

Revi sighed with pleasure and scanned the menu.

While they ate, Revi insisted on detailing everything she had read about investigating past lives. "If you go under hypnosis—"

"And how do you think I would manage that?" Emma demanded, irritated despite herself. "I can just see my dad's face if I asked for a hypnotist who specializes in past-life regression. He'd find me a psychiatrist, instead!"

"At least try some of the regression exercises in my book," Revi insisted, her mouth full of salad. "They sound really interesting, and—"

"Revi, I wish you would just drop it," Emma snapped. Even her food was losing its flavor. She reached for a roll, her movement so abrupt that she sent the bread rolling off the plate and over the side of the table. "Oh, now look."

"You can have mine," Revi said, her tone soothing. "Don't get mad, Emma. I think it's fascinating, having a psychic link to someone you never heard of."

"I do not have a psychic link!" Emma retorted, her voice rising. One of the women at the next table glanced their way. Emma lowered her voice with an effort. "I just—I just can't get her out of my mind, that's all."

"See, I told you."

"Revi!" To her horror, Emma found that her eyes were damp with sudden tears; she blinked hard, and her friend's expression of dismay was blurred.

"Okay, okay, I'm sorry, Emma." Revi sounded genuinely contrite.

Emma took a deep breath, trying to regain her self-control. She sniffed back the tears, then frowned at her best friend. "Easy for you to say. It's not your face that turned up in an old photograph!"

"I wish it were; I think it'd be cool to have a psychic connection—that is, never mind, I won't say anything else, I swear." Revi applied herself to her salad.

That resolution would last about ten minutes, Emma told herself. But she didn't have the heart to argue anymore. Anyhow, that was why they were in the city, to find out more about this mysterious person, this shadowy figure that had emerged from the past to haunt Emma's dreams and her daytime thoughts as well.

They finished their lunch without speaking; Revi was so quiet that Emma felt a stirring of remorse. "Want some dessert?" she asked, when one of the waiters walked by with a tray full of sumptuous sweets.

Revi looked undecided. "I don't know if I brought enough money."

"That's okay, I'll buy. My mom let me use her credit card," Emma said.

They shared a tangy fruit tart with whipped cream and a silk-smooth crème brûlée topped by hard-glazed caramelized sugar. They had done this since they were small—ordered two desserts and then split them half and half. Thinking of all the two of them had shared—they had been friends since kindergarten—Emma's anger faded as quickly as it had come.

When the waiter took the credit card away, Emma glanced at her best friend. "I'm sorry I exploded like that."

"No, I shouldn't have insisted—" Revi began.

"It's just that I'm scared," Emma went on, her voice very low. "I'm scared, Revi."

"Oh, Em." Revi's dark eyes were full of concern.

"I have this feeling that there's something terrible out there, just waiting for me—and it makes me cold inside."

Emma looked down and discovered she was clutching the napkin so tightly that her knuckles were white.

Revi put her hand on top of Emma's. "I'm here," she said. "It's okay, Em."

Then she withdrew her hand as the waiter returned with the credit card slip for Emma to sign. As they rose to leave the restaurant, Emma tried to tell herself that she was being silly.

When they walked out of the department store and headed for the bus stop, Revi draped one arm around her shoulders.

"Forget everything I said, okay? There must be some ordinary, boring reason for all of this. Maybe she's a distant cousin you never heard of. Your mom's from California originally, isn't she? Some relation there, that's the most likely answer."

"My mom's parents died a long time ago," Emma reminded her friend. "Even her grandmother, who raised her, died before I was born. Mom hasn't been back there in years. And I've never heard of any relations."

"Your dad's family, then," Revi went on. "There are lots of them."

"Yes, and they're all dairy farmers in Wisconsin," Emma argued. "Well, most of them; Uncle Don is a lawyer. But none of them looks that much like me."

Revi waved at a bus, and when it pulled in to the curb, they both climbed the steps and paid their fare. The seats were full, and Emma clung to a hand strap as the bus chugged its way back into the line of traffic. As they rolled along through the crowded city streets, Emma told herself that this time her friend had to be right. There was some ordinary, everyday explanation for the girl whose image haunted her. Emma just had to find it.

When they reached the library, Emma explained what she wanted, and they were directed to the third floor. She soon found herself at a microfilm machine, scrolling through roll after roll of old newspaper issues.

In the next booth, a grad student with a long ponytail trailing over his black T-shirt whistled merrily. Emma had glanced at the screen as she walked past; it looked as if he was viewing some obscure psychology journal. In half an hour, he had found what he sought, printed it out, and shoved the rest of his papers and books into his backpack, making an incredible amount of noise in the quiet room. Then he walked away, still whistling, his hiking boots clunking across the floor.

Of course, he knew what he was looking for. At her machine, Emma was having no luck at all. Another hour passed without success. Emma straightened and rubbed her eyes. She was chasing a needle in a haystack. Maybe she should give up now and admit that she was being totally wacko about this whole thing.

At least she wasn't alone, so she didn't feel menaced by the quiet or the empty corridors. Emma glanced at Revi, at the next microfilm reader, squinting as she stared into the viewer. With two of them, the search would only take half as along. And Revi hadn't complained at all about how long they had spent in the library, as if determined to make amends for upsetting Emma earlier.

Emma told herself she should turn off the machine and walk away, go shopping, have fun, enjoy the Saturday afternoon, and most of all, try to forget the ghost from the past that haunted her thoughts. But if she did, the first time she stared at her own reflection in a shop window, she knew what she would feel: a tremor of the fear that had become a constant companion. She had to find this shadow self who disturbed her peace of mind, who refused to fade away.

Taking a deep breath, she threaded another roll of microfilm into the machine and began again.

Almost another hour had slipped by before Emma saw

the photo. The headline had alerted her. "Protest Group Challenges Proposed Sale of Redwood Groves," the newspaper shrieked. And the photograph . . . if she hadn't already been attuned to the mystery girl's face and form, she would have missed it. This time, the blonde girl's expression was distorted with rage as she struggled in the confining grasp of a policeman. Behind her, other long-haired, T-shirted protesters appeared to have chained themselves to the large trunk of a towering redwood. But it was the girl who fought with the police who drew Emma's eye.

Emma chewed on one nail, her stomach churning. Who was this person, and what had brought about the anger on her face? Was her emotion all about saving the redwoods?

Emma's silence, the tenseness of her body as she leaned close to the screen, must have alerted Revi.

"What is it?" her friend asked. "Did you find something?"

Emma nodded.

Revi jumped to her feet and came to bend over Emma's shoulder. "Oh, man. It's her! And, Em—" Revi hesitated, but Emma knew she had something else to say.

"What?" Emma asked, her voice cautious. She braced herself at her friend's obvious reluctance.

"Well, you know. Saving the redwoods. Don't you remember last year, when you led that petition at school about saving the rain forests?"

"That's just a coincidence," Emma snapped, fear flooding her again. "It doesn't mean there's anything tying me to this—this stranger!"

"I didn't say there was," Revi said, her tone soothing. "It's just—just funny, that's all."

Emma wasn't laughing. She adjusted the viewer slightly to read the caption beneath the photo. And this time, this time the reporter had a name to identify the girl with Emma's face.

"Police subdue protestor Leigh River Greenleaf," she read aloud, her voice fading as Revi gasped behind her.

"That's your name!"

Emma shivered as if a wash of cold air had emerged from the past along with the photograph. Emma Leigh Carter—it was even spelled the same way. There must be something here—whether psychic link or more mundane distant kin, something about this girl tied her to Emma.

Emma read the article carefully, but there were no more details about this particular protester, only about the group, which had apparently had many protests and had already run afoul of the law.

Emma scanned the next year's newspaper issues and found one more mention of the Green Power group; this time, they were protesting a nuclear plant being built in Southern California, and again police had been called to break up the noisy demonstration. Several people had been injured in the melee that resulted.

"Don't seem to be too committed to nonviolence, do they?" Revi murmured. "They should have paid more attention to Dr. King's writings."

Emma nodded, but the lump in her throat kept her from answering. She pushed the button to print out this article, too, as she had with the first one. This time the girl she sought, Leigh River Greenleaf, was only a distant blur in a crowd of people, but Emma was sure of her identity; she was as attuned to this stranger as if all of Revi's theories of psychic connections were true.

Emma scanned more newspaper headlines, but although the group was mentioned a couple more times connected with environmental protests and mob violence, Leigh herself seemed to have disappeared abruptly. What had happened to the girl?

At last Emma pushed herself away from the machine, returned her rolls of microfilm to the reference desk and collected her printouts. Then she and Revi walked back to the bus stop without speaking.

Revi glanced at her cautiously. "Are you okay? Do you feel better now?"

Emma sighed. "I need to know more," she said. "I can't let it go, Revi. I have to know who this girl is."

Revi's expression was concerned. "But how?"

A city bus pulled in to the curb, emitting a black puff of diesel smoke. The door wheezed open and disgorged a knot of passengers. The girls climbed on and were soon headed back to the parking garage where they had left Emma's car. Emma finally answered her friend.

"I don't know."

California, she thought. That was where all the protests had taken place. The answers lay in California.

Dear Diary,

The police picked up Martin Morningstar. Martin shoved some guy, but so what, he had pushed Martin first. Martin isn't violent, not really, and believe me, I know the difference. One of the cops grabbed me, too, but I slipped away. He was distracted when one of the other guys smashed his sign over the cop's head, and he forgot about me. So I got away this time.

I don't want to be arrested again. They might lock me up for a long time, and I'm afraid of the small cells—they make me think of the times my dad locked me in the closet when I was too small to escape. It was so dark, and the smells—the smells made my stomach churn.

And worse, they might take me home. Dad might even be there, and if he is, if he knows the police have snagged me, he'll beat me again. I don't have time for broken bones—we have the big demonstration coming up, and I want to be there. I don't want to let Tony down. I have to be there!

Chapter
Four

On Monday, when Emma put her books into her locker, she saw the crumpled folder that detailed the summer classes offered by her private school. She pulled it out, a sudden memory igniting a spark of excitement deep inside her.

The sharp tone of the buzzer made her jump. She thrust the brochure into her textbook and hurried to class. But while the teacher lectured, Emma pulled out the papers and covertly scanned the list of classes. Yes, it was here! And today was the cutoff date; she had no time to waste.

She cut her next class and went to see the counselor instead. When she met Revi at lunch, her friend was frowning. "Are you sick? Cramps?"

"No." Emma slid her lunch tray onto the table. She wasn't sure how to tell her best friend what she had done.

But Revi's eyes narrowed as she saw the papers atop Emma's folder. Before Emma could stop her, she grabbed the top sheet.

"You switched your summer program! Emma, why?"

"I decided I wanted to do something different," Emma said, her voice a little too high-pitched. "Don't be mad, Rev."

"Mad?" Revi shrieked. "You've ruined our whole summer! We were going to do the dolphin institute together. Now I'll be all by myself. How can I go to the beach by myself? Are you pissed at me? What did I do to you?"

"No, no, I'm not mad," Emma tried to interrupt, but her friend continued her tirade.

"And why the heck do you want to study the history of cinema? You're not interested in movie making."

"I might be," Emma argued, not quite able to meet her best friend's eye. "We made that video in our speech class last year, remember?"

"I remember we did it together," Revi said bitterly. "I can't believe you've deserted me like this. Was it because of what I said about the psychic connection? You know you don't have to act like— Em, that's it?"

Emma looked away. "No, but—"

"I can't believe you'd hold a grudge like this. Emma, you're my best friend!"

"I'm not mad, I promise you," Emma said, her voice low. "Please don't be angry at me, Rev. I'm sorry we won't be together. You'll have fun anyhow, you know you will. You always make friends easily. You'll have every guy at the institute in love with you."

"But—"

"I just have to do it." Emma picked up a fork, then laid it down again; her appetite had died. "I have to."

Revi frowned, her expression puzzled, then she looked down at the paperwork again. "Los Angeles," she said, a long breath slipping out, her anger fading as quickly as it had come. "You're looking for your shadow twin. That's it, isn't it?"

Emma nodded. "I have to know; I can't stand it. I think about her all day and I have strange dreams that I can't even

remember when I wake. I just know that I'm scared—
something's wrong, somewhere. I have to find out what
the answers are."

Revi bit her lip, her tone quiet now, but still very
somber. "Emma, have you thought—"

She broke off, and Emma stared at her, waiting.

"What if you don't like the answers?" Revi finished
slowly.

Perhaps that was Emma's biggest fear. She shivered. "I
have to know," she said, not arguing. "I just can't stand
this—I can't even look at myself in the mirror."

Revi sighed and reached for her glass of soda. "What
did your parents say about this last-minute switch?"

Emma chewed on one nail. "I haven't told them yet."

"Oh, wow," Revi said. "That should be fun."

Emma didn't answer, but her stomach was already
knotted with tension. She pushed her plate away. What
would her parents say?

When she got home from school, Emma was frustrated to
find only their housekeeper at home. Sandy stood in the
kitchen, bending over the oven. "Take this out at five-
fifteen if your mom's not home," she told Emma.

Emma nodded. "Is Mom going to be late?"

"I don't think so, but I don't want the lasagna to burn,"
Sandy said sensibly. "Your brothers are at the park; they
should be home by five. I have to leave early; I have a den-
tist appointment."

Emma patted Happy absently while the little dog's tail
wagged furiously. "All right."

"Don't forget, now. The timer is set, but if you're up-
stairs, you won't hear it." Sandy untied her apron and hung
it in the pantry. "You okay, Emma? You look like you're on
another planet."

Emma tried to smile. "Just a lot on my mind, with
school almost over."

Sandy nodded. "Lucky you, all summer to have fun in," she pointed out, picking up her purse. "See you later."

Emma didn't feel lucky. She pulled a textbook from her backpack and sat down at the kitchen table to read a home-work assignment, afraid if she went up to her room she would forget the pasta dish. The smells drifting from the oven made her mouth water; her stomach felt hollow after eating so little at lunch.

Just before five, she heard her mother's van pull in, and she shut her book, rehearsing again all the convincing arguments she had practiced. When her mother came in with her arms full of groceries, Emma stood up quickly and went to help her.

"Down, Happy," her mom said, sidestepping the eager little spaniel. "Down."

Emma took one of the heavy paper sacks from her mother's arms; her parents refused to use plastic because paper was easier to recycle. "Are there more bags?" Emma asked.

"I'll get them; put the milk and yogurt into the fridge, please," her mom said.

Emma pulled out the cold cartons and put them away. Her mother returned with more bags, and together they put away the foodstuffs.

"How was school?" her mother asked, picking up several boxes of noodles and stacking them in the pantry.

"Okay," Emma said. "Um, I've decided to switch my summer class."

Her mother bent over to take out a bottle of olive oil. "Really, why?"

"I just decided this sounded more interesting," Emma said, hoping her voice didn't reveal her nervousness. "It's the history of film, and I thought—"

"In Tampa?"

The back door banged open, and her brothers pounded

inside, arguing loudly. "It's your turn to take out the garbage—"

"No, it's not—"

The dog ran back and forth between them, jumping at their legs and yelping, as if in chorus.

"No, it's in Los Angeles." Emma tried to get her answer in. "I thought the course—"

The timer on the stove went off, buzzing shrilly and drowning out her words. Emma's mother jerked, and the bottle of cooking oil slipped out of her hand, crashing against the tile floor. Emma heard the glass shatter and saw droplets of olive oil splatter across the tile. She gasped.

The two boys stopped to stare at the damage. "It wasn't me," Todd declared at once. "It's Ethan's fault."

Their mother sighed. "It's no one's fault," she said. "But you two quiet down."

She grabbed a roll of paper towels and knelt to attack the mess. "Emma, would you see to the oven, please."

"Sure." Emma grabbed two potholders and removed the big pan of pasta from the oven. "Smells good. I'm sorry about the oil."

"I should have been paying attention," her mother said, but her voice sounded a little strained. "Now, what's this about your class? Is it because of Revi—did she change her mind? I didn't know she was interested in movie making."

"No, Revi is still going to Florida to study dolphins," Emma admitted. "I just—I'm the one who thought the history of film class sounded exciting."

"But why? It's not like you to go gaga over celebrities. You don't have a crush on some movie star, do you?" Her mother sounded worried.

Emma was startled into laughter. "Of course not."

"I really don't think you should change your mind at the last minute." Her mother dumped a handful of greasy paper towels into the garbage can, then went back to pull more off the roll. "And it's not fair to Revi, do you think, after you two had planned to go together?"

Emma frowned. She felt guilty about leaving Revi, but she had to do this, she had to.

The back door opened again. She looked up in surprise to see her father coming through the door.

"Hello, ladies," he said, setting down his briefcase.

"You're home early," Emma answered, hurrying to his side. He put one arm around her and hugged her, and she smelled the familiar smell of hospital antiseptic that always clung to him when he first got home.

"He went in at five this morning," her mother pointed out, dryly. "I'm glad you're home, Russ. Emma wants to change her summer program."

"Oh?" He shrugged off his jacket and tossed it over the closest chair. "No dolphins? Now what is it?"

"A movie class," her mother said, before Emma could explain. "And I don't think it's a good idea."

"It's about the history of filmmaking," Emma said in a nervous rush. "Revi and I made a video for speech class last year, remember? It was fun; I just thought I'd like to explore the subject a little. I'll be making college plans, soon, you know."

"You're not going to the West Coast!" her mother said sharply. "We talked about Smith, even Harvard. The best schools are in the East."

"But Dad went to UCLA—"

"It doesn't compare to Harvard! And you shouldn't change your plans on such a whim," her mother repeated.

"She's only seventeen," her dad put in, his voice gentle. "I don't think she's going to ruin her life by trying a new interest, Beth."

"But so far away—"

"It's only for a month," Emma argued, her voice hoarse. She couldn't bear it if her mother said no.

"She's not going away for a year," her father agreed.

"Nor even for a semester—it's just a summer class. I think she should get it out of her system now."

"But—Los Angeles . . ." her mother repeated. "All the crime and drugs and—"

"Oh, Mother." Emma made a face. "You're overreacting. I'm not going to turn into a zombie and forget everything you've taught me for seventeen years. Can't you trust me?"

Her mother's expression twisted, but her father grinned back at her. He walked across to put his arm around her mother's shoulders.

"We know we can trust you," he said firmly.

Emma sighed in relief and picked up her backpack to slip out of the kitchen. It was time to leave her dad to argue with her mom, she knew from past experience. Her mother was usually levelheaded, but sometimes she got overprotective. Her father was always open-minded, and he was okay with her decision, Emma could tell, and he would probably prevail.

It was going to happen! With any luck at all, she would soon be on her way to the West Coast.

Chapter
Five

The last weeks of school flew by. Emma studied extra hard—partly to get the shadow girl out of her head—and breezed through her exams. She attended graduation, warm with pride as Jay made his speech, and later they went to the graduation dance, Emma resplendent in a new shimmering gold-toned dress that she and her mom had picked out together. The dress set off her pale hair, which she'd pulled up onto the top of her head, and she had long sparkly earrings that brushed her shoulders.

Jay whistled when he came to pick her up. "Wow! You look like a movie star, Em."

Behind him, she saw her mom glance worriedly at her dad, and she wished her boyfriend had picked any other comparison. Her mother was still unhappy about Emma going to Los Angeles, no matter how many times her husband tried to reassure her.

"Thanks." Emma let him drape her matching wrap over her shoulders. "You look very nice, too."

He fit into the dinner jacket as if he had never worn

anything else. Looking at his handsome face and polished smile, she had a premonition: Jay would go far in life; how could he not? Whether he became a politician or a businessman or an attorney, he would be a big success. And did he see her at his side? Did they have a future together?

She knew he would meet lots of girls when he went away to college in the fall, but still, they made a handsome couple, everyone said so. Both were tall and fair and clear-eyed, both had well-cut clothes, smoothly sculpted cheekbones and the grace that comes with years of sports and gymnastics and dance lessons.

She kissed her parents quickly, and she and Jay posed for pictures while her dad fiddled with his camera, saying several times, "Just one more."

At last Jay offered her his arm and took her out to the car. As he made a show of opening the door for her—"In you go, lady fair," she felt a thrill of pride, glad she was the chosen one, that out of all the girls at Oak Grove High, he had still picked her.

At the country club where the dance was held, they ate dinner, then danced and chatted and danced again, and for once Emma managed to forget—almost—the shadowy figure from the newspaper photo. Tonight, it was all now, all Emma and her boyfriend, Emma and her other school friends. Revi was dating a junior, so she wasn't at the dance, but there were plenty of girls that Emma knew, plenty of guys.

The evening spun away too quickly. When Jay drove her home, Emma hated to get out of the car, hated for the night to end. But if she lingered, Jay would only think she wanted to make out, and she felt too dreamy for that. It was the emotion she wanted to hold on to, the feelings of happiness that seemed somehow threatened by the clouds on her personal horizon, clouds of mystery, of unknown danger.

No, even tonight, she could not forget the face from the past.

When Jay kissed her good night, she didn't pull away, enjoying the firm touch of his lips, the spicy smell of the men's cologne that he preferred. When they finally drew apart, Jay was breathing quickly.

"Whoa." He grinned. "Trying to get my blood pressure up? Not to mention—"

She shook her head. "It was a wonderful evening," she said gently. "I'm going to miss you when you go away to college." She opened the car door, and he came around quickly to put one arm around her shoulders as she walked up to the house.

"Hey, I'll be back often," he told her. "Especially for kisses like that! And the evening doesn't have to end now, you know. I know a place—"

"No, I'd better go in," she said, evading his glance. She didn't want to fight with him, but she wasn't ready for anything heavy. "I don't want to cause trouble with my parents; my mom's still freaked out that I'm going off to Los Angeles. She thinks I'm going to be instantly corrupted."

Jay bent to kiss the curve of her neck. "So, we'll start the corruption early, while you're safely at home."

"Very funny." She kissed him again quickly, then turned and put her key into the lock. She could hear Happy yapping on the other side of the door as his shaggy ears picked up the sound.

"You'll be sorry," Jay said from behind her. "None of the kooks in La-La Land will strike your fancy—you've got too much good sense. Why did you change your class, anyhow? I thought you and Revi were into the dolphin thing."

"Just wanted to do something different," she said vaguely. She had answered this question before, and she still didn't have a very convincing explanation. "I'll see you before I go."

"I guess so," Jay said, still sounding disgruntled. "If I haven't withered away of frustration."

"Very funny," Emma replied. "Bye." She shut the door

firmly on his exaggerated grimace and leaned over to pet the dog, who frisked along beside her as she walked down the hall.

She found her dad in the kitchen, ostensibly making a cup of cocoa. She wondered how long he had been stirring the mug of milk; it looked as if the liquid had already cooled. But he always manufactured an excuse to hang around and see her when she came in—just to be sure she was okay.

When she had first started dating, it had annoyed her. Now she just smiled inside and pretended not to notice that he made a habit of waiting up.

"Dance all night, did we?" her father asked, his tone light.

"Just about," Emma agreed. "It was fun."

She gave him a quick hug, then ran lightly up the stairs, already putting the night and the dance behind her. She had only five days left before she winged her way to California—and all the answers that awaited her there.

Pausing in the doorway of her bedroom, Emma shivered suddenly. Was that a premonition of disaster? No, she was being silly, she told herself. Just excitement, that was all.

She closed the door behind her and tossed her evening bag onto her bed. As she slipped out of her dress, Emma tried to think about clothes, packing, mundane matters that would stop the rapid beating of her heart.

But after she crawled into bed, the dark thoughts returned like moths circling a streetlight. What if Revi were right—what if she found answers that she didn't want to know? Emma lay with the covers pulled up to her throat and stared unseeing into the darkness.

A car drove by on the street outside her house, then quiet returned, and she heard a owl call, mournful and low. Maybe she should drop the whole thing, cancel her film history class in Los Angeles, try to get back into the dolphin institute with Revi, make everyone happy—her best friend, her mom, even Jay, perhaps, who didn't understand her sudden change of plans any more than anyone else.

But then she would never know who the girl in the photograph was, the girl who had Emma's face. Could she live her life not knowing?

The silence stretched in the dark room, and Emma closed her eyes. It was a long time before the thoughts that whirled round and round in her head at last faded, and sleep came.

She filled the next week with last-minute shopping trips with Revi, impromptu dates with Jay, even playtimes with her brothers, sitting in front of the TV with their favorite videos, or challenging them to computer games that had all three shrieking and laughing until their mother came to see what was going on.

"Come on, Mom, you can play, too," Ethan said as their mother peeked around the door frame.

"I think I'm too old for this," she said, pushing her graying hair back behind her ears.

"You're not old, Mom," Emma argued, watching her mom's gesture. "But you should do something about your hair. It makes you look older than you are, you know."

It was an old argument. Her mother shook her head at the comment and accepted the control that the boys urged on her.

"Like this, Mom," Todd said.

"I'll never figure this out," their mother protested, but soon all four of them were laughing and shouting until the little cocker spaniel ran up and down the room, barking wildly. They were still there when the kids' father came in from the garage, sitting his briefcase on the floor and bending over to pat Happy, whose tail wagged rapidly.

"Who's winning?" he asked.

"Me," Todd said smugly. "Come and play, Dad. Bet you can't beat me."

"Heavens, I have to get dinner on," their mom said, wiping tears of laughter from her eyes. "You'll just have to save the universe without my help." She stood up and gave her husband a quick kiss, then headed for the kitchen.

The boys pulled their dad into the game. When they were called in to eat, Todd was still ahead.

"World champion," he told them. "No, galactic champion!"

Ethan made a face, but Emma laughed, and their dad grinned. "Come on, champ, your mom says dinner's ready." They walked into the kitchen together.

After dinner, Emma and her brothers cleared the table and loaded the dishwasher, then Emma swept the floor before going up to her room. She pulled her suitcase out of the closet and began her packing.

Sunday morning she woke early, a shiver of excitement deep in her stomach. For a moment, she stared at the familiar blue-stripped walls and tried to remember why she was so tense, her shoulders already rigid with suppressed emotion. Then she remembered: Today was the day.

She clicked off the alarm and went into her bathroom, turning on the shower. The warm water needled her skin and sent her adrenaline level even higher. She was on her way, and somehow she was sure that everything would become clear once she got to the West Coast and had the chance to ask questions of the right people, dig into the right databases.

After she dried her hair, pushing the sleek shimmering mass of it back behind her ears, she pulled on a favorite pair of jeans and a new short-sleeved cotton sweater in a delicate aqua shade that set off her greenish-blue eyes; they looked especially vivid today in her face because she was pale with excitement. She took her suitcase and backpack downstairs and ate a bagel while standing at the kitchen counter, too keyed up to sit.

When she finished, she sipped a glass of juice and waited impatiently for the rest of the family to get downstairs. She had wanted her dad to drop her off at the airport, no fuss, no commotion, but her mother had wanted to come, too, and then her brothers. Emma was pacing up and down, glancing at her watch when the boys finally got downstairs.

Emma patted Happy, rubbing the little dog's ears as he tried to lick her hand. She gave him one more pat, then went to the garage and climbed into the van, followed by her brothers.

"Keep it down, you guys," her dad said.

The ride to O'Hare seemed long to Emma, but soon they were turning into the airport exit and approaching the long terminals. Her parents had agreed to let her walk in by herself, so her dad pulled the van up to the curb and got out to take out her luggage. He took it over to the baggage pickup and stood in line, waiting for the skycap to check it.

The boys peered out of the windows, watching for planes.

"Bye, guys," Emma said. "Behave yourselves while I'm gone."

"Ha," Todd said, "not likely."

Ethan looked wistful. "I'll miss you, Emma," he declared.

Touched, she leaned into the backseat to hug him, and reached for Todd, who ducked away from her kiss. "I'll be back soon," she promised.

Her mother got out of the van, too, to hug Emma. Her blue eyes looked sad, and her expression was hard to read.

Emma felt a wave of contrition; her mom couldn't help being overprotective, that was the way she was made. And Emma didn't want her to worry. She tried to tell her so. "I'll be fine, honest. And I'll be home in a month."

Her mother reached one hand to touch Emma's hair, her caress light. "I know. Be careful," she said very low.

Emma hugged her mom, leaning into the comfort of her arms as if she were small again. "I will," she promised.

"Call us when you get to the dorm," her mother ordered.

"Emma," her dad called. "Come and show the man your ID."

Emma turned away, but the last glimpse of her mother lingered in her mind's eye; her mother still looked sad, maybe even frightened.

Emma dug out her student ID to show the skycap, then her suitcase was tossed onto a cart. Her dad held out his arms, and she hugged him.

"Be smart," he told her, kissing the top of her head. "And call if you need us."

"I will," she promised. She knew that he meant not just in class, but in the choices she made. Emma felt a sudden shiver of fear of the big world, the strange city she was going to all alone. But it was too late now. She straightened, smiled at her dad, and pulled her backpack onto one shoulder. Holding her ticket firmly, as if it were a talisman, she waved at her family, then headed inside the airport.

The airport was crowded with people. Emma made her way through the crowded walkways, stood in line to go through the security check where she surrendered her backpack to go through the X-ray machine, and walked through the metal detector, where her belt buckle set off the alarm and she had to tug the belt out of her jeans and go back through again.

Hastily tucking the belt back through her belt loops, she picked up her backpack and hurried on. She found her gate, but the waiting area was already crowded, and she saw no empty seats. Emma paced impatiently up and down until the plane began boarding.

She had flown often with her family, vacations to New York to visit museums and Broadway shows, jaunts to scenic New England villages, summer trips to a cabin on the farther reaches of Lake Michigan. Planes didn't scare her; it was the destination that made her heart pound faster.

As soon as she could, Emma boarded the plane and found her row. She took out a magazine and small bottle of water, then pushed her backpack into the overhead storage bin. When she settled into her seat, she turned to gaze out the small, thick-paned window.

She watched men loading luggage into the plane, and technicians scurrying as they readied the plane for the cross-country flight. She thought about Revi, who would be boarding a plane herself in three days and flying to Florida. Emma felt lonesome, suddenly. It would have been much more fun to go with her friend. At least Revi had finally forgiven her for changing her plans. When they'd said good-bye, Revi had gazed at Emma soberly. "I hope you find what you're looking for, Em," she'd said. "I hope by the time you come home, you can forget you ever saw that girl in the photo."

The mystery girl who had started it all, Emma thought. She had tucked the wrinkled photos carefully into her backpack; she knew them all by heart now, every grainy inch; she didn't even have to look.

When the door was sealed, the flight attendants began their safety lecture. Emma listened for a minute, then glanced out the window as the engines revved. As the plane pulled onto the runway, then paused, she felt a surge of impatience. Go, she wanted to say, go, go!

At last, the plane rolled along the runway, picking up speed. Emma watched the blur of movement out the window, and when she felt the small lift as the plane rose off the ground, her stomach clenched in excitement. This was it!

As the city fell away beneath them, she leaned back in her seat and thumbed through her magazine, but she was too distracted to read. After a while, the flight attendant brought soft drinks and juice, and a small sandwich with a half-inch of lettuce and some type of mystery meat. Emma nibbled at the edges, then put it down and ate her tiny cup of pasta salad and her cookie. No wonder her mother had become a vegetarian.

The day was clear and the skies very blue. Sunshine

glinted in through the small window, and Emma had to adjust the pull-down shade to cut the glare. Emma stared out the window, watching the miniature landscape below until they had crossed the Mississippi River and were high over the flat Kansas plains. Then she dozed—she had been too excited to sleep much the night before—and didn't wake until the plane bumped and shook as it negotiated moving air currents like a frail canoe on a swirling river.

Somewhere behind her, a baby wailed. The businessman next to her snored gently. Emma rubbed her eyes and peered out the window again; the flat lands of the country's interior had been replaced by mountains; she could see brown ridges, traces of snow, and farther down, the feathery greenery of tree lines.

Soon, the plane began its descent. Emma's ears popped, then plugged up again. She searched in her pocket for some gum and chewed vigorously to open up her ears.

Now she could see a city ahead, an enormous expanse of houses and palm-lined streets and occasional backyard pools. Freeways and narrower avenues, crowded with tiny cars and trucks, dissected the megalopolis. The city sprawled across the foothills and then flowed on across the flatter ground as if it had exploded outward, expanding from the ocean into the hills and deserts and touching the very hem of the mountains themselves.

It looked very different from Chicago's neat green suburbs and outlying corn-rowed farmland. Emma stared out the window, her excitement returning. Here was where she would find the truth about the shadowy twin who had emerged from the past.

Here she would finally lay the ghost to rest.

Chapter
Six

When she heard the grinding sound as the plane's landing gear descended, Emma's heart beat faster. Now she could see the glint of ocean waters at the far side of the great metropolis, and she had glimpses of larger buildings and always, the ever-present freeways, crowded with cars. Where were all those people going? Emma wondered absently.

The speaker hummed, and the flight attendant spoke again. "Please be sure all tray tables are stowed, and all seats are in their upright position."

Emma straightened her seat and watched as the plane dropped even lower. Now she could see the airport, the small buildings and planes and service vans growing larger as her own jet plunged earthward. Closer, closer, then the runway rushed up to meet them, and the plane hit the ground with a jolt. It taxied along the pavement, gradually slowing as Emma drew a deep breath.

She almost shivered with impatience, waiting for the plane to roll up to its gate, waiting for the seat belt sign to go dark, at last standing and grabbing her backpack out of the overhead bin. Then more waiting until the line of people ahead of her surged forward, and Emma could take long strides toward the door. She hardly noticed the flight crew at the front of the plane bidding passengers good-bye; she was too eager to plunge into the tunnel connecting the jet to the airport building.

When she emerged into the terminal, Emma walked on past small groups of family reuniting with hugs and exclamations. For a moment, it made her feel alone, but she shrugged the thought aside. She had very specific directions on how to get to the college dorm, and her parents had gone over it with her several times. And she had traveled before without her parents, Emma told herself firmly. Okay, last time she and Revi had been together, but still—

She paused in the congested hallway to look for signs that pointed to the baggage claim, then walked down to wait for her suitcase to emerge from the chute and join the rotating belt of luggage. When she spotted her bag, she pulled the suitcase off the conveyer belt and headed for the door. A line of people waited for their luggage to be checked against their luggage claim sticker; Emma pulled her ticket out of her backpack so she could get through the check site, then emerged at last into the open air.

Looking around, she drew a deep breath. She thought she could detect a faint hint of salt air—how far was Los Angeles International Airport from the ocean? The air was unexpectedly cool. She shivered in the breeze that swept through the airport drive and then hurried to find a taxi.

When she had secured a cab, and the driver had picked up her suitcase and lifted it into the trunk, slamming it briskly, Emma climbed into the backseat, holding onto her backpack.

"Where to?" the man asked, his accent heavy. He wore jeans, a T-shirt, and a Dodgers baseball cap and had a straggly black mustache; he looked like an escapee from an outlaw gang, but Emma hoped appearances were, in this case, deceiving. She had the card with instructions in her jeans pocket, but she had the address for the college memorized, and she rattled it off with a very adultlike calm, she thought proudly.

The driver nodded and turned back to face the road; he pulled the cab into the traffic with a jerk that made Emma grab the edge of her frayed seat and look around for a seat belt. Her mom was very big on seat belts, and Emma had promised her parents to act sensibly.

When they pulled away from the sprawling airport, Emma blinked at the busy city streets around them. The sunlight itself seemed brighter, and pale wispy clouds hung at the edge of the blue sky. Where was the smog she had read about? Today, at least, it seemed to have disappeared. She stared at the tall buildings, the crowded streets, the sidewalks thick with people of all ages and sizes and nationalities. Within two blocks, she saw a man wearing a turban, a woman draped in a colorful sari, and a street person pushing a rusted grocery cart heavy with blankets and bags.

Emma blinked, and again, for a moment she wished she were not here alone. But she had to do this, she would do this, and soon she would be home again, sharing all her stories with Revi and Jay—well, some of them with Jay. She had never told her boyfriend about the picture, the girl from the past who had Emma's face. She wasn't even sure why not, it just seemed too—too private, too personal, perhaps too scary. Jay liked everything explained, ordered, planned. He wouldn't have approved of her dashing off across the country to track down a tantalizing photo from years ago, just because her intuition told her that she should.

When they reached the college campus, the driver told her the total she owed, and Emma remembered to add a tip, again feeling very adult. Outside the cab, the driver retrieved her suitcase, dropped it on the sidewalk, then got back into the taxi and drove away.

"And thanks to you, too," Emma muttered. But she pulled her suitcase along, looking for signs to direct her. She was impressed with the campus itself, mellow with sun-bleached stone and dotted with palm trees and other greenery. College students could be seen occasionally strolling along the sidewalks or draped across a bench, chatting, reading a book, or listening to a Walkman, their expressions far away.

After a couple of false starts, she found her way to Royce Hall, a Gothic-looking building with tall towers, and found a sign inside that directed her to the summer program desk. There, a friendly blonde woman wearing a bright red tunic top helped Emma sign in and gave her directions to student housing.

Emma signed the forms, picked up a packet of scheduling and orientation pamphlets, all the while feeling a little guilty. She had come here for another reason, after all, but she would try to enjoy the film course, too.

She walked back outside and eventually found the building to which she had been directed; her room was on the first floor, a tiny cubicle with twin beds and a battered double desk. At first glance, Emma thought no one else was here, but then she heard whistling and saw a petite girl almost hidden inside the closet.

"Hi," Emma said, feeling suddenly awkward. "I'm Emma."

"'Lo." The stranger straightened and pushed back a mass of curly dark hair. "I'm Sophie, your roommate. Where you from, Emma?"

"Chicago." Emma dumped her backpack onto the empty bed and pushed her suitcase against the wall; this room was so small she wondered how on earth they would both fit without falling over each other.

"Wow, first time in L.A.?"

Emma nodded.

"You'll have fun, don't worry!" Sophie said. Her voice was musical and held just a suggestion of an accent—Hispanic, Emma thought. "We got nothing to do this afternoon, hey, I can show you around."

"That would be great," Emma agreed, grinning with excitement.

"What you want to see?" Sophie asked. "Want to go down to Venice Beach, or the shops in Santa Monica are cool, or—"

"What I'd really like to visit," Emma interrupted, "is the *Los Angeles Times* building."

Sophie stared at her.

"I have some research to do," Emma added weakly.

Sophie shook her head. "All work and no play, huh? I can see you gonna be some fun roomie." But she softened the comment with a grin.

After Emma called her parents and reported an uneventful trip and safe arrival, the two girls took a bus downtown and found the large light-toned building that housed the newspaper, but the security guard inside the lobby told them that the archives were closed at this hour. Emma, to her frustration, found herself very quickly back on the sidewalk.

The wind gusted and made her shiver; a tattered piece of newspaper slid along the pavement and a car honked as a man jaywalked across the crowded street. She had an absurd desire to sit down and cry; she felt very lost and alone and too far from home. With an effort, she pushed back her sagging shoulders.

"Too bad," Sophie said, her glance curious. "That important, huh?"

Emma tried to soften the disappointment that she knew must be obvious in her expression. "No, I'm just—just impatient, I guess," she said slowly. "I should have thought to call first. I'll come back another day. At least I know how to get here now. Thanks for coming with me."

"Sure." Sophie glanced up and down the street, where the fading sunlight cast deep purplish shadows. "I think most of the shops are closed, too. Want to get something to eat? I'm starved."

"That sounds good," Emma agreed. "I'm hungry, too." And she was, realizing suddenly that some of the emptiness inside her was purely physical. The inadequate lunch she'd been served on the plane had faded away long ago.

"I know this great Indian restaurant not too far from here," Sophie said. "You like Indian food?"

"I don't know," Emma admitted. "But I'm willing to try it."

"Good." Sophie grinned again. "Come on."

They ate curry and rice in a tiny restaurant heavy with exotic odors, sitting at a small table crammed close to the other patrons. Around them, Emma heard a babble of polyglot tongues, at least a dozen different languages, a score of different accents. One woman at the next table had blue hair; a man beyond had three rings in his eyebrow. Emma tried not to stare. She felt as if she had landed on another planet, not just in another state. Perhaps Los Angeles had a bit of many countries in it, she thought. Or perhaps other universes, as well, she added, grinning to herself.

She felt no connection to this strange place at all. Revi's theories about Emma's psychic connection to the girl in the photo seemed more and more like a tasteless joke. Perhaps she had given up a fun trip with her best friend and sabotaged a great summer for no reason; likely the girl with her face would turn out to be just some strange coincidence, Emma told herself.

If only she could really believe that was true.

She took a bite of curry and coughed as the spicy food burned her tongue. She reached for her glass of Coke, but Sophie grabbed her hand.

"No, eat some bread; that works better."

Emma nodded, tearing off a bit of thin leathery bread and eating it quickly, then wiping away the tears that dampened her lashes. "Wow."

"It's good, though, once you get used to the spices," Sophie said, her tone encouraging.

"If I have a tongue left, I might agree," Emma said dryly. But still, it was fun to try something different. Jay would be impressed when she told him about this adventure, she thought. Her boyfriend liked to appear cosmopolitan and sophisticated.

She glanced around at the colorful decor and cautiously took another bite of the searingly accented dish, building up a slow acquaintance with the pungent foods they had ordered. She would give L.A. a fair chance, though her stomach might never be the same again.

"Tomorrow," Sophie said around a bite of bread, "I'll take you to a real Mexican restaurant."

"I've eaten Mexican food," Emma told her. "At least I'll be better prepared for that."

"In Chicago?" Sophie tossed her dark hair back and reached for a piece of bread. "I don't think so!"

They took a bus back to the campus. Sophie turned aside when they started down the walkway. "Here, I'll show you a shortcut." She led the way into a concrete stairwell, opening a metal door at the bottom.

Surprised, Emma blinked at the shadowy corridor that lay beyond. "What is this?"

"A service tunnel," Sophie explained. "They're all over, beneath the campus."

"Is it safe?" Emma shivered as they walked faster.

"Umm, I don't know if I would use them by myself, but with two of us, sure."

Then they were climbing another set of steps and emerging only a few yards away from the dorm building.

Back in their room, Emma unpacked her suitcase, propping a small photo of Jay up at the side of her desk.

"Your man?" Sophie asked. She had sprawled across the other bed with a book in front of her. "He's hot."

"He's going to Yale this fall," Emma said. "But we're still going to be a couple."

"Huh, maybe," Sophie murmured. "My brother went off to Stanford and dumped his girl. 'Course, she'd already found another dude, so it was just as well."

"I think we'll make it," Emma said, giving Jay's handsome face one last look, then she took out the textbook that went with their film course and sat down to read the first chapter.

She had to at least pretend to be interested in the class she had flown across country for, Emma reminded herself. No one else had to know that she had an ulterior motive. She didn't want to come across like a total crazy.

Probably, she thought, remembering the strange people she had seen—the street people looking for handouts, the woman in the orange robe collecting money for some unknown charity, the man who'd looked stoned out and glassy-eyed though it had been barely dusk—L.A. had enough crazies already. Had her mother been right all along about the dangers of a strange city?

None of it would influence her, Emma promised herself. She had one purpose here, and she would do her research, find some boring and prosaic answer to her puzzle—she hoped—and go home again. Remembering Jay's comments, she grinned slightly. She had no intention of being corrupted, of being changed at all. She would go back the same Emma who flew out, having lost only a few taste buds and maybe gained a few new clothes. She was not in danger here, despite her friends' and family's concern.

But when they turned out the light, despite the fatigue

that dragged at her whole body, she was too keyed up to shut her eyes.

Emma listened to the unfamiliar sounds of traffic and blinked at the light that filtered in through the sagging blinds at the window. Her bedroom at home was so quiet, with only the occasional car passing outside, so peacefully dark and safe. But she was being silly. There was nothing dangerous here, she reminded herself once more. Yet, when she finally closed her eyes, the dreams came again.

Dear Diary,

Dad came home drunk again tonight. I heard the scratchy sound he makes when he can't quite get the key in the lock. He kicked the door and swore and I knew he'd yell at me, or worse, for locking it. But I get so scared all by myself.

Outside, sometimes men hang out on the corner, selling little packets of drugs, and once I saw a man wave a gun around, yelling at the drug dealers. So I locked the door after Dad left, and tonight I fell asleep in front of the TV and I didn't hear him in time. So it was too late to open it before Dad tried the knob, and I knew he'd be mad. I couldn't run and unlock it because I didn't want to be close enough for him to grab me.

Instead, I ran for the kitchen and climbed up on the counter so I could slip outside the window onto the fire escape. It was cold, but I had a sweater, and with luck, he would forget about me and go to sleep, and then I could

*crawl back into the apartment, go to bed and lock my bed-
room door.*

*But he had to be asleep first, or—drunk as he was—he
could still kick in my door . . .*

Chapter
Seven

Emma woke once in the middle of the night, a loud sound outside the building jerking her out of her sleep. For a moment, she blinked in confusion, totally disoriented. This room was too small to be her bedroom, and the sounds outside were too loud. Then she remembered where she was, and she tried to grasp the memory of the sound that had shattered her dreams. Had it been a gunshot?

She strained to hear, her whole body tense as if she were under siege, but she detected only normal traffic noises. Across the room, she could heard the faint rhythm of slow breathing as Sophie slept peacefully. Sophie hadn't awakened. She lived here, she would know what was normal and what was not.

Probably it had only been a car backfiring, Emma told herself. She was just jumpy because she was in a strange place, that was all. She turned over and thumped her too-thin pillow, trying to make it into the right shape and size, like her pillow at home. The sheets supplied by the linen service were too scratchy, and the blanket too heavy.

A sudden rush of homesickness washed over her. She wanted to be at home in her own bed, with her own things around her. She wanted her pesky little brothers to be asleep down the hall, and to know that her parents were a comforting presence in the master bedroom. She even missed her dog, who would snuffle and lick her feet if she poked them outside the covers, tickling the sensitive instep until she laughed aloud.

Why had she come here? It had been a stupid idea. Maybe she should forget the whole thing and fly home. If she went back now, she might be able to join Revi on her trip, and they would have fun on the Florida beaches, just as they'd planned.

But she couldn't. The girl in the faded photo would still haunt her. Why did Emma have bad dreams she couldn't quite remember—what was it that pulled her toward this stranger? She didn't know; she just knew that she couldn't walk away.

Okay, she would find out as much as she could, and then she'd leave early. She'd tell the teacher here she had an illness at home, and she'd tell her parents she'd gotten homesick. It might be too late to join Revi—well, maybe just for a week or so—but Jay would be there, and she'd have her comforting world back, her family, her friends, the place where she belonged.

And no matter what Revi had speculated, that place was not here, not this strange city with its multitude of ethnicities, its tongue-searing food and busy sidewalks, packed freeways and palm trees that swayed in ocean breezes.

L.A. might be a nice place to visit, but Emma didn't want to live here. She wanted to go home.

Having made a plan, of sorts, she felt a little better. The tension in her body faded, and her eyes closed once more.

When the travel alarm sounded, she struggled to reach it. Across the room, the covers on the other bed lay tumbled; Sophie was already gone. Emma pulled on a robe, picked up her toiletries bag and went off to shower. After a quick bagel, she hurried to her class.

The instructor was young and had a ponytail; the students were a mixture of skin color and accent, some from Los Angeles and many from across the country. Emma discovered she was not at all the farthest from home, but that didn't make her feel more at ease. One girl had even flown in from France, and most of the teens seemed intent on studying filmmaking, as aspiring directors or screenwriters or even actors.

After a brief introduction, the instructor passed out some handouts. The teen in front of her turned to pass her the stack of papers and she glanced at his face. He had dark hair and a strong nose; he wasn't smoothly handsome enough to be an aspiring actor, she thought, although it was a pleasant face, with eyes a clear blue-gray, sparkling with intelligence. Maybe he was one of the budding directors.

He looked at her as well. "Hi, you local?"

"No, Chicago," she said. "You?"

"Bay Area," he told her.

When she looked blank, he added, "Outside San Francisco. I'm Luke Fulton."

"Oh." She nodded this time in understanding. "Emma Carter. Are you serious about the film business?"

He grinned. "As serious as anyone can be. I've already gotten one spec script written, and half of another."

Emma blinked, impressed. "Good for you."

"What about you?"

Emma hated to admit she was, in a sense, crashing the class under false pretenses. "I—uh—made a video at school last year, and it was fun. But I don't know if I'm going to study filmmaking; I'm just investigating the possibilities."

"Makes sense," he said, and to her relief he didn't look disdainful.

Then the instructor cleared his throat, and Luke turned

to face the front of the room. The other students quieted, too, and settled down to listen.

The teacher talked about the first films made in California, after early filmmakers had come west because of more prevalent sunlight. "Not so much smog then," he told them, and the class laughed. "And these guys had no big lights, no special cameras; every reel was shot in open air and sunlight, and they didn't need cloudy or rainy days to stop their shooting."

It was an interesting subject, and Emma forgot to be distracted. The instructor lectured for an hour, then after a short break, they watched a Charlie Chaplin silent film, and then discussed it. Emma said little, but she enjoyed the lively discussion. Still, by the close of the two-hour class, Emma felt restless, sneaking covert glances at her watch. The film discussion was interesting enough, but she had come here for another purpose.

When the class was dismissed, Emma headed straight for the bus stop and waited for what seemed like a small eternity until the right bus pulled in.

Sneezing a little at the fumes in the air, she paid her fare and found a seat, holding her backpack on her lap. Today the air was heavier, the skies gray with a semilucent haze that must be the L.A. smog she had read about. As the bus chugged along, she watched the crowded streets, clogged with cars and trucks and vans, and didn't wonder that the air was thick with their collective exhaust.

When she reached the right street, Emma jumped down the steps and hurried to the newspaper building. This time, she made it past the receptionist and on to the archives section and was soon ensconced in several reels of microfilm.

For three hours Emma stared at the small print on the screen, scanning for more stories about the group to which Leigh River Greenleaf had belonged. Among the columns of fine newsprint, she found articles detailing half a dozen protests, some of which had erupted into noisy brawls that had to be broken up by the police.

Emma read each piece carefully and found two more mentions of the Leigh River Greenleaf she was searching for, brief comments, a line or two only, in the midst of the stories of protests and civic disturbances. Then the girl from the past seemed to disappear abruptly. The group itself continued to be mentioned in the newspaper articles for a couple more years, then it faded away. But the girl with Emma's face had disappeared abruptly and without a trace.

Emma pushed herself away from the microfilm viewer with a feeling of total frustration. This couldn't be all, it just couldn't. She hadn't come all the way across the country just for this!

Maybe she'd been a fool, Emma thought. She'd ruined her whole summer for nothing.

Her shoulders sagging in discouragement, Emma collected the few news articles she'd printed out, stuffed them into her backpack, and then wandered outside the building. She didn't know what to do now.

She tossed her backpack over one shoulder and walked aimlessly along the pavement, glancing into shop windows, hearing the constant whine of traffic in the street, dodging the other people who thronged the sidewalks.

She couldn't have come this far for nothing. There had to be answers here, somewhere. What was she missing?

The sun was warm on her face. When her legs felt tired and the weight of her backpack pulled at her shoulders, Emma stopped and sat down on an unoccupied bus bench. She folded her arms across her chest and shut her eyes, almost sick with discouragement. What was she doing in an alien city, so far from her family and friends? She didn't belong here.

But as she half-dozed, tired and disheartened, the street sounds around her seemed to slip inside her thoughts: cars and trucks rolling along, fragments of conversation as people walked past her down the sidewalk, the occasional stray seagull shrieking overhead, pigeons cooing and fluttering as they worked the grimy sidewalk looking for crumbs. She could smell the acrid scent of the exhausts and catch an occasional whiff of exotic foods from the tiny restaurant behind her. And for an instant, in her state of half-consciousness, it no longer felt alien and strange.

It felt like home.

That thought jolted her wide awake again. No, no way, Emma told herself. Nothing in Los Angeles was familiar, in no way was she connected to this new city, this patchwork of streets and communities that she had glimpsed on the plane ride in. It was only a fanciful thought, that was all.

She stood up, no longer willing to rest here, feeling somehow vulnerable. She looked around, wondering if she were totally lost. She walked along the street until she found a drugstore that sold maps, bought a city map and opened it, leaning on the counter until she could figure out where she was in relationship to the university.

Then she went back to a bus stop and waited for a bus heading in the direction of Westwood. When she stepped off the bus, she made her way back to the campus with only one wrong turn—Emma had always had a good head for directions—and somewhere during her long walk, her mood changed.

She was here, for better or worse, in one of the nation's great vacation spots. Stop whining, she told herself. Have some fun, for crying out loud. Then, if she decided to go home early, at least the trip wouldn't be a total loss. Her parents had paid a lot for her plane ticket and for a class she was barely interested in.

So when she found Sophie in the dorm room getting ready to go to dinner, Emma nodded when her roommate called, "There you are, girl. Want to come and eat with us?"

She joined a group of classmates, and together they walked to a small Mexican restaurant where once again

Emma's taste buds were challenged to new heights of spicy heat. The food was good, though fiery by Midwestern standards. Emma drank several glasses of water and cola to ease the burning in her mouth and throat, but she agreed when Sophie raved about the dishes.

"The best you'll find north of Baja," Sophie said seriously.

Emma took another sip of water, but she grinned and nodded. "I'll take your word for it," she said, surprised that she could still talk.

Luke had come with them, a girl from Arizona named Kizzy, and a guy from New York. The other teens all talked briskly about films and Hollywood and how to best break into a cliquish industry. Most of the group had plans to attend UCLA later on.

Emma listened, trying not to betray her relative ignorance of the entertainment industry, and once in a while she thought about her boyfriend at home. What was Jay doing right now? Had he asked someone else out, some other girl, while she was gone? If he did, he did, she told herself, pushing the thought away. No point worrying about it, and certainly nothing she could do to stop him. But she might call him tonight, Emma told herself.

When they finished dinner, the New York guy, Alan, wanted to go look for a club that might let them in despite their age.

Luke shook his head. "I haven't read my chapters for tomorrow's class yet," he said, "and I'm beat."

Emma wasn't in the mood to party, either, so she walked back to the dorm with Luke, while the rest of the kids went the other direction, looking for more action.

"What did you do this afternoon?" he asked her as they waited to cross a busy street.

Emma shrugged, feeling defensive. "Some research." She hoped he wouldn't ask for details; she did not intend to tell anyone the real reason that had brought her to California. At last the light changed, and they strode quickly across the street. "What about you?"

"Went to the beach," he said. "Did a little body surfing."

She glanced at him in surprise. Somehow, he didn't look the type.

He must have read her thoughts. "Oh, I'm not a dedicated surfer," he told her. "But it's fun, once in a while. Ever tried it?"

"In Chicago?"

"Point taken. But a group of us are going back to the beach tomorrow after class, if you want to come," he invited. "You don't have to surf, just relax on the sand, swim a little, you know."

He grinned, and she found herself relaxing. "Sure," she agreed. "I could use a break."

When they got back to her dorm, Luke said good night and headed for his building. Emma went along the hall to her own room and unlocked the door.

Before tackling the reading assignment, she dialed Jay's number. The phone rang, and she felt a flicker of relief when the connection was made, but it wasn't Jay's voice she heard.

His mother answered instead. "Oh, hello, Emma. How's Florida?"

Emma grimaced. "I'm in California, actually," she told Mrs. Lewkoski.

"Oh, I thought— Well, how's the class? Are you enjoying the dolphins?"

"It's interesting," Emma said, sighing. She didn't really want to explain about the class change. "Is Jay home?"

"No, dear, he's gone out. Can I take a message?"

Emma felt a wave of loneliness. "Just tell him I called, please." She gave Jay's mom the number at the dorm and waited for her to find a pencil to write it down.

"I'll tell him. Have fun in Fl—in your class, dear."

Frowning, Emma replaced the receiver. She felt very alone, and very far from home.

Chapter
Eight

Shaking her head, Emma took out her textbook and forced herself to read the chapters they'd been assigned. As long as she was here, she didn't want to look like a total idiot in the class discussions.

That night, she slept heavily, with no dreams that she could remember, and the next morning in class, she tried her best to pay attention. She laughed at the clip of the Marx Brothers the instructor showed, and then blinked at the skewed drama of *Birth of a Nation*, which led to a lively discussion afterwards of the role film should play in showcasing controversial topics, even biased viewpoints.

After a quick lunch, she rode the bus to the beach with Luke and Sophie and a group of teens from her class, glad she had packed a bathing suit in her suitcase. She bought a cheap beach towel from one of the shops, then walked down to the sand and spread it out, pulling off the T-shirt and shorts she had worn over her suit for the bus ride. She took a bottle of suntan lotion from her bag—her fair skin burned all too easily—and spread it thickly over her body, tying her long hair into a ponytail to keep it out of the way. Then she sat on her towel and watched the people on the crowded beach, while the rhythmic pounding of the waves against the sand eased the tension that still lingered inside her.

Near her, a small girl sat beside her mother and dug in the sand with a plastic shovel, and two boys ran up and down, tossing a ball back and forth. They reminded her of her brothers, and again she felt a wave of homesickness. Emma pushed the feelings back. She was going to have some fun, she told herself firmly, no matter how short this visit turned out to be. She refused to return with nothing but bad memories.

Luke and Kizzy ran past her, tossing a Frisbee. "Come on, Emma," Luke called, sending the disk flying her way.

Emma laughed and jumped to her feet, catching the plastic circle just in time. She threw it back, then ran along the sand, dodging family groups to snatch the Frisbee when it arced through the air toward her once more. Jumping over a snoring man with a pink balding head, Emma made the catch, exclaiming in triumph.

"Better," Luke said, his tone friendly.

"Better than what?" Emma asked, a little out of breath. She tossed the Frisbee toward Kizzy, who missed the plastic disk and ran to retrieve it from the water's edge.

"Better than sitting and brooding," he told her.

Emma blinked. "I wasn't—"

But Kizzy sent the Frisbee sailing back toward her, and Emma never finished the sentence. Still, she was determined to disprove his words. After the game ended, she dug out her camera and took some pictures. Then she walked down the sand and into the water, enjoying the cool splash of it against her body, the ebb and flow of the waves that rocked her almost off her feet and made swimming in the ocean so different from the placid waters of a pool, or even the mild swells of a lake.

A larger than usual wave swept over her head, drenching her and burning her eyes. Gasping, she swallowed water. Emma sputtered and spit out the salty seawater. A few feet away, Luke laughed at her expression. She tossed a handful of floating seaweed toward him, and he ducked.

He dove into the water, disappearing from her view. In a moment, she felt someone hook her feet out from beneath her, and she fell backwards, splashing for a moment as she sank, then pushing herself up to tread water.

Sticking out her tongue at him, Emma swam farther into the deeper water. Another wave came in, and she felt the strong pull of the undercurrent trying to tug her back out toward the horizon, toward the endless miles of ocean. She swam hard against it, for a moment alarmed at the strength of the current. While she floundered, her heart beating fast, Emma felt someone touch her arm, a strong, gentle touch that steadied her and helped her resist the pull of the undertow.

"You okay?" Luke surfaced beside her, his wet hair sleek against his head, beads of water rolling down his cheeks. He blinked against the saltwater and regarded her with concern.

"Yeah," Emma said, flushing a little. "I can swim pretty well, it's just—"

"Swimming in the ocean is different." He finished her thought. "You'll get the hang of it, don't worry. And the undertow is bad today. I wouldn't go very far out myself."

His candid admission eased her embarrassment. With Luke beside her, she no longer felt afraid. They swam for a while, sometimes ducking beneath the waves, sometimes letting the swells push them toward the beach.

Luke showed her how to body surf, which made Emma laugh and gasp as her first attempts sent her tumbling through the water.

Eventually, they went back to the beach and sat on their towels. Her mouth dry, Emma found her water bottle and drank some of the tepid water, then pulled the tube from her bag to reapply her suntan lotion.

Overhead, two seagulls shrieked, then dived toward the sand as they spotted a fragment of someone's discarded sandwich. One bird grabbed the bit of food and then flapped away, while the second bird protested angrily.

"Want me to do your back?" Luke offered after she had coated her arms and legs and face.

She hesitated for a moment, but his tone was matter-of-fact, and the other girls were still in the water.

"Sure," she said, handing him the tube.

He knelt behind her and rubbed the sun-warmed lotion over her bare back. His hands felt warm and smooth against her skin, gliding easily over the hollows of her back. The sensation sent prickles of feeling through her.

Hey, Emma had to remind herself, you have a boyfriend at home. Don't even think about—about the directions in which Luke's touch is sending your thoughts.

She hoped her face hadn't flushed. Maybe he would think it was only the sun.

But when he came to sit beside her, she shut her eyes and murmured, "The water always makes me sleepy." She felt suddenly shy, and she pretended to doze until the other kids rejoined them. But in fact, Emma didn't feel at all drowsy; she was acutely aware of Luke sitting a few feet away on his beach towel, of his broad shoulders and well-toned body.

Sophie sat down on her other side, shaking droplets of water toward Emma as she pushed back her heavy mass of wet hair. Sophie wrung out her thick hair, then toweled it briskly. She pushed through her own bag for a hair clip to hold it out of her face, and then reached back inside to find her watch. She frowned when she saw the time. "We'd better go if we want to get back before dark. Anyhow, I'm famished."

"Me, too," Luke agreed.

The sun had dropped low in the sky, sending its last brilliant beams glinting off the ocean, making Emma squint when she looked westward. Already, the temperature had dropped a little, and the winds from the sea were cool against her body.

Kizzy and Alan had joined them, and everyone was toweling off and dressing. Emma pulled her T-shirt and shorts over her almost-dry swimsuit, then stood and shook out her towel, trying to get off as much of the sand as possible. She folded it and tucked it into her backpack, picking up her sandals.

They walked up the soft sand until they reached the sidewalk, then made their way back to the bus stop. By now, Emma felt empty, too, and suddenly tired. As she trudged along the walkway, she passed another girl with long blonde hair, and for an instant, Emma's heart beat faster.

Then she saw the stranger's face; no, she looked nothing like Emma. And anyhow, the girl in the photos would be much older now, not a teenager any longer.

Besides, Emma had promised herself not to think about the girl from the past; she would not ruin any more of her summer in futile searches. Why spend her time in dusty archives when she could be on the beach?

As they reached the street, she spotted a display of postcards in one of the shop windows. Maybe she should send some cards to Jay, and Revi, and to her family, of course.

While the others walked half a block on toward the bus stop, Emma ducked into the shop. She quickly selected half a dozen cards from the rack, pulling money out of her wallet to hand to the clerk. "Oh, and stamps, too, please," she added.

"Hurry up, Emma, the bus is coming," she heard Luke call.

She grabbed the paper bag, took the change the salesclerk offered, and ran to rejoin the others. She reached the bus in time to climb the steps just behind them.

On the bus, Luke had saved her a seat beside him. Sophie watched them from the next row, grinning a little, and Emma avoided her roommate's eye. Sophie knew about the picture of Jay on her desk back in the dorm room. Emma didn't mean to give the wrong impression. It was all casual, just a group of new friends hanging out. Was that so wrong?

But she still felt a little disloyal, wondering how she would feel if Jay were out somewhere right now, lounging on the shores of Lake Michigan with some other girl. If it was as innocent as this, she wouldn't care, she told herself.

They piled off the bus when it reached Westwood and picked a small Italian restaurant for dinner. They ate spaghetti and salad, talking and laughing.

"We'll give Emma's taste buds a break tonight," Kizzy suggested, rolling her pasta onto her fork.

"Oh, I don't know," Sophie said. "Trying out something new can be fun." Her grin was impish, and she glanced sideways at Luke as she spoke.

Emma frowned at the other girl. "I know what I like," she said pointedly, hoping that Luke was picking up none of the extra levels of the conversation.

While the others talked, she finished her dinner and pulled out her postcards. Jay's card, at least, she would get into the mail right away, as if that would alleviate some of her guilt. She scribbled a quick message on the back of one of the cards.

Dear Jay,
    The film class is fun—but how hard is it to watch old movies? Hope your college-prep classes are going well. I miss you! See you soon.

                                        Love,
                                        Emma

As they walked back toward the campus, the girls stopping now and then to gaze into shop windows, the two guys talking about sports and walking slightly ahead, Emma spotted a small post office.

"Just a sec," she said. "I want to mail my postcard to Jay."

"It's closed," Kizzy pointed out. But when Emma tried the door, she found the outer lobby was open. She ran in to slip her postcard through the slot, then glanced at the bulletin board at the side, covered with yellowing posters and flyers. Suddenly she froze, her hand still extended toward the mail slot.

The postcard slipped out of her hand and fell to the floor. Emma hardly noticed.

At the top of the bulletin board, a faded photo had captured her eye. It was Leigh River Greenleaf, the girl from the protest group, the girl with her face.

And she was wanted by the FBI!

Chapter Nine

For a moment Emma struggled to take a breath; she felt as if she'd been body-slammed, struck harder than any of the waves today had pummeled her. Stiff with shock, she forced herself to take a deep, slow breath and read the poster again.

She hadn't imagined it. The face was there, Emma's face, the shadow twin with whom Emma had become so familiar during her search through old newspaper clippings. The girl's expression was even more defiant than usual: the mouth hard, lips pressed tightly together, the eyes narrowed in distrust. She looked angry and rebellious and frightened.

And the name underneath the photo was the same: Leigh River Greenleaf. What was the charge?

Emma's gaze dropped to the bottom of the flyer, and what she read there made her gasp. WANTED FOR MURDER, it read in bold letters.

Emma thought she might faint.

Behind her, she dimly heard a voice speak, but the

words made no sense; her mind was frozen in horror. This couldn't be true, she told herself. This girl, this girl who looked so much like Emma—

"You okay, Emma?" she heard Sophie ask. "What's up?"

"Um, nothing," Emma turned, panic-stricken. She didn't want her roommate to see the poster, observe the strange resemblance.

"You dropped your postcard," Sophie pointed out.

Emma bent over, her head spinning, and fumbled for the card. She straightened to push it through the mail slot, then took a quick step toward the door, almost stumbling. She wanted out of here before Sophie, too, glanced at the picture on the wall, noticed the strange resemblance.

"What's wrong?" Sophie asked again.

"I—I'm just tired, that's all," Emma muttered.

"Too much time in the water," Sophie guessed. "It can sneak up on you, sometimes."

They walked back to the dorm. The other teens talked quietly, but Emma paid no attention. She was still rigid with shock.

She remembered that she had felt a vague sense of threat, some dark cloud connected with the strange coincidence of the stranger who looked too much like her. But this—this was worse than she had ever dreamed of.

When they reached the residence hall, Sophie went down the corridor to Kizzy's room to look at some reviews of Kizzy's last acting role. Grateful for the silence, Emma collapsed onto the hard mattress of her twin bed, trying to think.

She couldn't panic, she had to think logically—that was what Jay would tell her to do. For a moment, she thought of calling him again, hoping she could catch him at home this time and pour out the whole story. But no, she didn't want to tell anyone, not until she understood more about this whole strange affair.

She had to stay calm; she had to think. Don't panic, she told herself; use your brain.

What had she missed, in her search through the newspaper files for her shadow self? Obviously, she had overlooked a major story. The first step was to go back to the newspaper, Emma told herself. Go back and find out why the girl with her face stood accused of murder—still stood accused.

It had all happened almost two decades ago, she reminded herself. Why had the girl never been prosecuted? Why was a poster of her shadow self still hanging on a post office wall?

That night, Emma tossed and turned, tangling herself in the covers while the springs of her bed protested with rusty squeaks until she was afraid she would wake Sophie. Not until the darkness in the room lightened and pale dawn light seeped past the crooked blinds did she fall into a restless sleep.

She woke to find Sophie touching her shoulder.

"Wake up, girl, you gonna be late to class."

"I'm not going," Emma muttered. "I don't feel so good."

"Want me to call the residence advisor?" Sophie asked. "You need a doctor or something?"

"No, I just want to stay in bed a while," Emma said. "I'll be okay, it's probably just a bug."

"S'okay," her roommate said. "I'll check on you later."

Sophie left for class, and Emma dozed for a few more minutes. Then she opened her eyes and blinked at the travel clock on her desk. She pushed back the covers and pulled on some clothes—she had showered the night before to get the salt off her skin—and was soon headed downtown toward the *Times* building.

She was becoming very familiar with this journey. Soon she was seated once again at a microfilm reader, scrolling through a stack of reels. And she found the story almost at once.

She had been too focused on headlines about environmental protests in her earlier research—that must have been why she had missed it. This headline blared: "Explosion kills bank guard," and the subhead said, "Robbery attempt led by Green extreme leader."

Emma made a small choking sound and tried to turn it into a cough. A middle-aged man sat at the next microfilm machine; she didn't want anyone to notice her. The grainy newspaper photos that accompanied the story showed a man and a young woman—Leigh, the girl with her face—and Emma felt a sinking feeling inside as she read the column.

A man who called himself Tony Cleanair Blueskies had been the leader of Green Power, the extremist environmental group; he had been mentioned in the earlier articles, but she had focused too narrowly on Leigh River Greenleaf to pay much attention.

According to the news story, Tony had gone into a large branch bank in Los Angeles with a note demanding money and a package he claimed was a bomb. The teller had given him a sack full of money from her till, but when he turned to leave, a bank security officer had accosted him. There had been a struggle, according to the surviving eyewitnesses, and then an explosion.

Tony and the bank guard had both been killed, and several bank employees and customers had been wounded, some severely. If Tony had carried the bomb, why was Leigh listed as an accomplice? Emma pushed back a strand of blonde hair and read on quickly.

A girl with long pale hair had been seen standing at the doorway of the bank, apparently waiting for the bank robber to emerge with the money. She'd also had a duffel bag slung over one shoulder, witnesses said, and at first, it was feared she'd also carried a bomb. So no one had dared to approach her, and in the confusion after Tony's bomb exploded, she had gotten away.

Emma found her stomach pinch with bewilderment and fear. Now this girl with her name, her face, was not just a violent protestor, she was a thief and an accomplice to murder. The knowledge made Emma feel literally ill. She pushed her chair back from the microfilm reader, feeling smothered, suffocated. She had an urge to jump up, run out and hide somewhere amid the crowded L.A. streets—almost as if she were the girl the police were still chasing.

Get a grip, Emma!

She shut her eyes for a moment, pressing her palms against her eyelids as she tried to control her churning stomach. She thought she might be ill right here. She had to be rational. This has nothing to do with you, she told herself. You're being stupid.

But at the deepest level of her instinct, she knew that somehow, in some way, it did. There was a connection; she just hadn't found it yet. And now she had to know what the link was between this girl and herself; she could never walk away now—not when the stakes had been raised so drastically.

Opening her eyes again, Emma drew a slow, deep breath, willing herself to be calm. She looked back at the screen; the black-and-white news photo showed the devastation that the bomb blast had wrought in the bank, shattered windows and twisted door frames. Emma could almost smell the acrid scent that must have lingered over the lobby, the curls of smoke from the resulting fire. And she imagined she could hear the screams of the victims—it had been a crude, homemade bomb, the newspaper said, with nails inside that had exploded outward when the blast came.

They'd had to identify Tony from his dental records; he'd had no face left.

Emma felt her stomach roil again and had to swallow

hard. She looked back at the photos of the two suspects, the dead bomb maker and the girl who was considered his accomplice. How had they taken the photos if the man had been blown to bits?

She read the captions beneath the pictures; both of the photos had been taken earlier, police IDs shot when the two had been charged after a protest months before. So the photos predated the bank robbery and explosion; the newspaper had probably already had them on file.

Emma finished the article and scrolled ahead looking for more stories. In the next several days the hunt for Leigh River Greenleaf was mentioned several times. Many of the protest group had been hauled in to the police station to be questioned—the bank guard who had died had been a former policeman and Emma deducted that the police had taken his death very seriously. The other protestors had claimed ignorance of the robbery scheme, but two of the group had been prosecuted, two women named Karyl Meadowlark Johansson and Tonya Save-the-Eagle Clearwater. Leigh River Greenleaf had not been found.

Emma searched through the following weeks of newspaper issues until her neck ached from leaning over the machine and her earlier headache returned with even more force. But the stories faded away, the protest group—left without a leader—had eventually broken up, and Leigh River Greenleaf seemed to have vanished completely.

At last Emma turned off her machine and returned the reels of microfilm. Shoulders aching, she made her way back down to the street.

She walked along the pavement feeling tired and discouraged. What had happened to her shadow twin? How could the mysterious girl have disappeared so thoroughly? With the local police and the FBI both searching for her, how could one nineteen-year-old, cut off from her friends, with no apparent backing from any other terrorist group that the Feds could detect, have eluded authorities? And, if the poster on the post office wall was correct, was still eluding them.

The Los Angeles sidewalks were crowded with people; it didn't seem so hard to think that one person could slip out of sight. But without money, without friends or family to go back to—how could she have lived?

Maybe she hadn't.

Was she dead? Had Leigh been hurt in the explosion—she was standing very close to the bomb blast, according to the reports—and the others on the scene had been too frightened and confused to notice her afterwards? Had she run away to die in some back alley, bleeding and alone?

Emma shivered at the thought. That would explain why the girl had never resurfaced, why no one had found her, heard of her. Yet, wouldn't the police have been notified, wouldn't someone have found a dead body? Unless Leigh had run so far, gone to some remote place outside the city, into the desert or mountains, before she collapsed. . . . It could have happened.

She should let it go, Emma told herself. Accept that answer, and go back to Chicago, forget all about this whole thing.

Yet, would the bad dreams continue, the dreams she could never remember when she woke? How long could this shadow self haunt her?

Emma stopped at a tiny Japanese noodle shop and ordered some plain noodles, then strolled along the pavement, eating the soft food absently, trying to ease her pounding head and the aching emptiness inside her belly.

She reached a bus stop and waited with the after-work crowd. When a bus packed with passengers finally pulled up to the curb, she pushed her way on. She had to stand and cling to a metal post, swaying as the vehicle rumbled along. She rode back to Westwood, got off the bus and walked along to the residence hall just as the sunlight was fading.

"Hey," Sophie called as Emma entered the room. "I was getting worried 'bout you. Did you decide to go to the clinic after all? Feeling better?"

"A little," Emma said, ignoring the first question.

Fortunately, Sophie had her mind on other topics. She sat at her desk applying mascara to her long lashes. "You missed a great class," Sophie said. "Dr. Petwee showed more films, and we got an essay to write. I brought you the handout with the directions."

"Thanks," Emma said, taking the sheet Sophie handed her.

"Bunch of us are going over to a teen club Alan heard about, if we can find it. Want to come?"

"I don't think so, thanks anyway." Emma shook her head. "I'm not up to it, not tonight."

"Yeah, you should get some rest," Sophie said. "You look like a deflated balloon." With that comforting comment, Sophie put away her makeup and headed for the door. "Bye."

Emma nodded. She glanced at the essay topic, then put the sheet down. What else could she do? How could she find Leigh if the combined strength of the FBI and the police had failed?

Emma took her backpack and dumped onto her bed all the printouts she had made of the old news stories. She sat cross-legged while she combed through the flimsy papers, looking for any small detail, any clue she had overlooked. After all, she had missed the biggest story of all—the attempted bank robbery and the explosion and resulting deaths. Perhaps she had also overlooked some other vital piece of information.

But if so, it didn't seem to be here. One of the problems was the obviously fake names. Emma shook her head at the list she had made of the members of the protest group who had been mentioned by the newspaper. Many of the group seemed to have assumed earth-friendly aliases that would not help her research if she wanted to track them back to earlier days.

Nobody was named River Greenleaf, Emma thought, wrinkling her brow, unless maybe they were Native American, and the blonde-haired, fair-skinned Leigh did not look the part. Maybe her parents had been unreformed hippies, but it was more likely—given the names assumed by the other protestors—that she had made up that name to reflect her mission.

Which left Emma wondering where to go next and how to proceed. After an hour of peering at the printouts, Emma put them aside and wrote a short essay for the film class. She knew it wasn't her best work—her thoughts were still far away—but she at least had to go through the motions. She didn't want to get kicked out of the summer class; that would blow her excuse for being here, and she wasn't ready to leave, not yet. Impossible as her search appeared, she refused to give up.

So the next morning, she attended class and handed in her paper. But she took little part in the class discussion and tried not to glance too openly at her watch as the two hours crawled by. When the class was dismissed, she picked up her backpack and headed for the hall.

"Emma, wait up," someone called.

She turned and saw that Luke hurried to catch up with her. "We're going back to the beach this afternoon, want to come with us? We can try body surfing again; you were just getting the hang of it the other day."

For a moment, Emma was tempted—she thought of the cool water splashing over her body, and Luke's hand reaching to steady her when she faltered—then she shook her head. "Can't," she said. "I have some research I have to do."

"For what?" he asked reasonably. "Our next assignment isn't due till next week."

"It's—um—family research," she invented quickly.

"You could work at the library later," he suggested. "And still come to the beach this afternoon."

Emma bit her lip. "Not today," she said slowly. "I really need—want to do this now. But—but ask me again the next time you go, okay?"

"Okay." She thought he sounded genuinely disappointed, and it warmed her. She had been feeling so alone, so separate in her self-imposed isolation that Luke's friendly smile was like a lifeline. Impulsively, she reached out to touch his hand—his skin was warm against her own—and then, as he was about to speak, just as quickly stepped back.

"Have fun," she said, turning away before he could answer and almost running out of the hall. Outside the classroom building, she slowed her steps and considered. She had meant to return to the newspaper archives, even though she had searched in vain the day before for more mentions of Leigh River Greenleaf.

But she remembered the poster in the post office—it had had more information, and Emma had been so shocked, she hadn't taken note of it. First she would walk back to the post office and get all the data off the WANTED poster, then she would go to the university library and see what she could find.

Emma stopped to buy a sandwich and ate it as she walked back to the branch post office. Today the post office was open and busy with patrons. She made her way as inconspicuously as possible—she still had a compulsive fear of being linked to Leigh—to the bulletin board and examined the poster more carefully. *Leigh River Greenleaf*, the poster said. *Also known as Leigh Grimble, formerly of 574 Juniper Street.*

Emma stepped aside and scribbled the name and address on the bottom of one of her printout sheets, then hurried out of the crowded lobby and back into the fresh air.

. . . *Formerly of 574 Juniper Street.* What if she went to

this Juniper Street—would anyone there still remember Leigh? It was worth a try. She took out the Los Angeles map she had bought and scanned the tiny lines that crisscrossed the map. Los Angeles had a lot of streets. This would take forever to find—no, dummy, there was an index. She scanned the street names until she found what she sought. There were a bunch of Juniper streets. Maybe this was just another wild-goose chase. She'd probably spend all afternoon on a hot bus, when she could have gone to the beach with Luke and the others, Emma told herself crossly.

But did she really want to find Leigh, or not?

She sat for several minutes studying her map and a bus schedule from her new student packet, checked her wallet for change and enough dollar bills, and then pushed herself up from the chair.

All she could do was try.

Chapter
Ten

Emma rode across town, switching buses twice and often asking the bus drivers for help. When she stepped off the bus, she looked around in dismay. Big blank buildings lined the street, which was almost deserted. She searched for a street number on the nearest building, then shook her head. Not even close. Was this the wrong Juniper Street?

She seemed to have ended up in a warehouse district; she glimpsed big containers stacked nearby, heard the grind and roar of heavy machinery as the huge metal boxes were moved and sorted. The narrow street where she had stepped off the bus was almost empty; only an occasional large truck rolled by, and she saw few pedestrians. A couple of men in work clothes and hard hats eyed her with open curiosity. "Hey, missy, you lost?"

Emma shook her head and turned away, feeling very vulnerable; she hugged her arms to her chest as if for protection. After a quick scan of the area, she hurried back to the bus stop, counting the minutes, her shoulders stiff with tension. She breathed a sigh of relief when at last a bus pulled in. She got on quickly and paid her fare, eager to get back to a more populated part of town.

This was not the smartest way to find what she was looking for, Emma told herself. First, she needed a better map, which might save her a lot of wasted time and keep her out of areas she knew her parents would caution her about.

When she reached another neighborhood closer to downtown, with crowded sidewalks and shops and restaurants lining the pavement, Emma got off again. She walked until she found a bookstore with a whole rack of Los Angeles area maps and bought the biggest one she could find—it looked like a phone book, thick with pages. Then she headed for the small café attached to the bookstore, bought a soft drink and a scone, and sat down at one of the tables to scrutinize the pages.

This time, she singled out a likely Juniper Street, where the street numbers seemed to match the location she sought. Feeling better prepared, she finished her scone, took one last sip of her drink and then walked outside to find a bus stop.

After another bus ride and a short walk, Emma located the street, and then walked several more blocks. While busy enough, this neighborhood was nothing like the Westwood streets around the campus with their attractive shops and numerous restaurants.

Here, many of the buildings looked slightly rundown, and the shops she saw were small, with grimy, print-smeared windows. She saw Korean markets, Mexican taco shops, and a Vietnamese café. The air smelled like spices, and always the acrid scent of smog hung over the street.

Her heart beating fast, Emma walked quickly along the pavement, searching for the street numbers. At last she came to the 500 block and she slowed to make sure she didn't miss 574. But there was a gap in the numbers; Emma walked up and down the block several times, but the site she wanted wasn't there.

At last she picked a building at random, a small bakery. A bell dinged as Emma went inside. The tiled floor was in need of repair, but the air smelled sweet with the odor of baking, and the paper-lined shelves looked clean. If she hadn't already eaten a scone, Emma would have been tempted by the cookies and cakes and pastries lined up on the shelf.

She could always take something back to the resident hall. Anyhow, she needed an excuse to talk to the teenaged girl behind the counter.

Emma walked closer and scrutinized the baked goods.

"Can I help you?" the girl behind the counter asked, smacking her gum. She had olive skin and dark hair, and her white apron was spotted with dots of icing.

"Two of the fruit tarts, please," Emma decided. "And half a dozen of those cookies. Your family own the bakery?"

The girl laughed as she took out a small white paper box and reached for a set of tongs. "No, I just work here."

"Is the owner here?" Emma asked as she watched the salesgirl carefully pick up two of the fruit tarts and place them into the box, putting the cookies into another.

"Naw, she's gone to the bank." The girl glanced at her curiously. "That'll be eight-twenty. Why you want to see the owner?" She handed Emma a white bag with the baked goods.

"I'm looking for the Grimble family—I think maybe they're cousins of my mom. Someone told me they lived on this block; I thought this might be the place." Emma tried to keep her voice casual as she handed a ten-dollar bill over the counter.

The salesgirl laughed as she counted out Emma's change. "I think someone told you wrong," she said. "The owner's name is Chang, and she sure don't look much like you."

"Oh," Emma said. "She's owned it a long time, then?"

"I don't really know." The girl popped her gum. "You'd have to ask her."

"Sure, thanks," Emma said. She walked slowly out of the shop, carrying the bag. She felt absurdly disappointed. It had been a long shot, she told herself. She asked more questions in all the stores along the block, but without luck. Sighing, Emma stopped at the street corner. Then she had an idea. She slipped off her backpack and dug into its depths, searching for her small camera. She turned and snapped several shots of the street and the shops on either side. Just in case, she told herself. When she finished the roll, the automatic camera whirled and buzzed as the film rewound, and she tucked it back into her bag and headed for a main street where she could find a bus back to Westwood.

When she got off the bus again, she stopped at a drugstore advertising one-hour film development and left her film, sitting on a bus bench until the film was processed. Then she walked back to the resident hall and unlocked the door to her room.

The other side of the room was empty; Sophie was out somewhere. Emma let her backpack slide to the floor, then dropped on to her bed. She lay back against the blanket, shutting her eyes and letting some of the tension drain away. She had been hiking across a strange city, going to places her parents would never approve of, and she had found out nothing. Some detective she would make.

Thinking of her family made Emma realize that she should call home; she'd only spoken to her parents once since she'd arrived, and that was—how many days ago? Four? It seemed forever. Maybe it was time to tell them about her strange quest—or maybe they would think she'd lost her mind and order her home at once.

She dialed and listened to the phone peal, impatient for someone to pick it up. At last, someone answered. "Hello?"

Emma said. "Mom?"

"It's me, Todd," her brother said. "Emma, that you? What you up to?"

"Not much," Emma said. "Are Mom and Dad around?"

"Yeah, maybe," Todd said.

"Find out, lunkhead," Emma said. "I want to talk to them."

Instead of putting down the phone to follow her instructions, her brother said, "I think you should come home, Emma. Dad's worried—"

"But I'm doing fine," Emma interrupted. "I haven't done anything dangerous. It's just that—"

"You're not the only person on the planet," her brother retorted. "I didn't say it was about you."

"Then what?" Emma wrinkled her nose, puzzled, wishing she could see her brother's face. Was he just being a brat, teasing her over nothing? Or was something really wrong?

"It's Mom," Todd said, and this time she heard a telltale quiver in his voice. "Dad's worried about Mom; I think he thinks she's sick."

"Why?" Emma knew that her own voice had sharpened. "What's going on?"

But this time, infuriatingly, Todd did drop the phone with a clunk that hurt her ears. She heard faint voices, then a deeper voice came across the line.

"Emma? How's the film class?"

"Hi, Dad," Emma said, relaxing a little. "Lots of fun. Is everything okay? What's wrong with Mom?"

"Probably nothing," her dad said, his tone easy. "She hasn't been sleeping well, and she's lost a little weight."

Emma felt her fingers tighten on the phone. She thought

of cancer and heart disease and all those terrible diseases that filled the hospital beds with patients. "Is she sick?"

"I want her to get a checkup, but I'm sure it's nothing serious," her father repeated. "What about you? Seen anything of Los Angeles?"

"A little," Emma answered. "I've been to the beach with some of the kids from my class. I'm learning to body surf. My roommate is from Los Angeles, so she knows the city."

"That's nice," her father said.

Emma felt suddenly homesick again, wishing she were back home waiting for Jay to pick her up for a date, shooing her brothers out of her room, seeing for herself that her mom and dad were okay. "You'd call me if you found out any—any bad news, wouldn't you?"

"Sure, honey, don't worry," her father said in a reassuring tone. "Just enjoy your class and the new friends. We miss you."

"I miss you, too." She felt a tightness in her throat.

"Whoops, my beeper's going off; I better call the hospital and find out who needs to speak to me," he told her. "Love you, pumpkin."

"Love you, too," she said, then hung up the phone receiver slowly. Only then did she remember that she had told her family nothing about the mystery girl, the girl from the past who had her face. Maybe it was just as well. Her dad had enough on his mind, and she didn't want to worry her mom.

Emma pulled out her textbook and resolutely read the homework assignment, after a few minutes reaching for the bakery bag and eating one of the fruit tarts. The cream filling was smooth and sweet, the kiwi and peach slices on top appropriately tart.

When she had finished the two chapters, Emma shoved the textbook into her backpack and pulled out the snapshots she'd had developed. A few she'd taken earlier at the beach, but the end of the roll held the photos she had shot on Juniper Street.

She looked through the pictures slowly, searching the street scenes, the faded shop fronts, not even sure just what she was looking for.

Then her eyes narrowed, and Emma drew a deep breath. On the small dry cleaners three doors down from the bakery, a faded sign read: JOHANSSON CLEANERS.

If she remembered right—Emma leaned over and grabbed her backpack, pulling out the sheaf of newspaper files she had copied. She thumbed through the stack, looking for the right one. Yes! The two protestors who had gone to jail after the bank robbery and explosion: One had been named Karyl Meadowlark Johansson.

Emma stared hard at the photo of the thin-faced, dark-haired girl. The newspaper article said she was twenty years old; Leigh had been nineteen. The only physical similarity to Leigh River Greenleaf was the sullen expression on her face. But Leigh had been connected to Juniper Street, too, and these young women had been in the same organization.

Tomorrow, Emma was going back to Juniper Street. Perhaps it had not been such a dead-end after all.

The next morning was Friday; Emma was not the only person to fidget and glance at her watch as the class wound to a close. Many of the other teens apparently had partying on their mind. When the class ended, the classroom emptied rapidly. Emma hurried toward the door.

Luke stopped her on the way out of the classroom. "Any plans for the weekend?" he asked.

"Um, not exactly," she hedged. "I'm doing some—some more research this afternoon."

"Oh. If you decide you'd like to go to the beach tomorrow, let me know." He handed her a small slip of paper. "Here's my room number and phone."

"Thanks," Emma said, pushing it into her jeans pocket. "That's nice of you. Maybe I will."

He relaxed just slightly. "Hope to see you later."

Emma thought about what a nice smile he had all the way to the bus stop. But on the bus, as she was jostled by a broad lady with three shopping bags, Emma's thoughts returned to more serious topics.

Could she locate Karyl Johansson? If this was a family business, would they know where she might be found? Emma stepped off the bus when it reached Juniper Street and walked rapidly until she came to the dry cleaners. Pausing for a moment on the street to get up her nerve, Emma pushed open the door. A bell jingled as she stepped over the threshold. The air inside was warm, with strong smells of cleaning fluid and a hint of steam from the laundry in the back. The woman at the counter glanced at her, then back to the baldheaded man who was complaining about his suit coat.

"But I specifically told you the stain was coffee, and look—you didn't do a thing about it. How can I wear the coat looking like this? It's my best suit!"

"We'll do it over, Mr. Olson, and this time, I'll be sure to spot clean it first. Maybe the part-time boy didn't mark it."

"I can take my business somewhere else! You know how long I've been coming here? Fifteen years, that's what. I should think you could do a better job for such a good customer."

The woman made more soothing comments until the man finally dropped his spotty coat on the countertop and stomped out.

Emma gave him a wide berth and then cautiously approached the counter.

The woman looked tired; she pushed dark hair streaked with a few strands of gray away from her face and barely glanced at Emma. "Yeah? You got something to pick up?"

"Um, no, actually." Emma took a deep breath, not sure how to approach the subject, then blurted out, "Do you know a Karyl—spelled with a 'k' and a 'y'—Johansson?"

The woman blinked, then pulled at the shapeless cardigan that hung round her shoulders. "I don't think so."

"But this is a family shop, isn't it? Maybe there's someone else here who would know Karyl, know where she is now, I mean?"

"There's no one else here," the woman retorted, her voice sharp. "And I got no time to waste. I think you should leave!"

She grabbed the coat the man had left behind and disappeared inside the inner door, leaving the outer room empty.

Emma felt her face flush. She'd never been thrown out of a business before. Her chest tight with embarrassment, she turned abruptly and walked out into the cooler air of the street.

She smelled diesel exhaust and Chinese food and the tinny odor of the omnipresent smog. She felt like a fool. She took several aimless steps up the street toward the bus stop, her only thought to get away from this place. Then she stopped so abruptly that a woman pushing a baby stroller almost ran into her.

"Sorry," the woman said, her accent thick.

"Excuse me," Emma said politely, her mind racing, and her humiliation forgotten. She turned on her heel and almost ran back to the laundry.

Inside, another customer stood at the counter. "Now don't shrink the sweater," she was saying. "It was a birthday gift from my aunt."

"Not to worry," the dark-haired woman said. She glanced up at Emma, her expression closed and her eyes hostile, but she didn't comment. Emma held her breath until the customer left, then she stepped closer.

"Look, I told you—" the woman began, her tone belligerent.

"I saw the name tag," Emma said clearly.

The woman's hand flew to her breast, then she stuttered, "W-what name tag?" But it was too late; her action had given her away.

"The tag you pulled your sweater over and tried to hide when I was in here before," Emma said, feeling her pulse jump and her mouth go dry. "The one you're not wearing anymore. The one that reads, *Karyl*."

Chapter Eleven

The woman—Karyl Johansson—shut her eyes for a moment and sighed. "What's this all about, anyhow? You a reporter?"

Before Emma could answer, Karyl opened her eyes and stared hard at Emma's face. "No, you're too young. My God, is this for some school report—have I ended up being a footnote in a sophomore term paper?"

"No, you don't understand—" Emma tried to interrupt, but the older woman wouldn't listen.

"Look, it was a long time ago, okay? I'm through with that part of my life. Why can't you just leave me alone? I don't want to be in any more news reports or 'where are they now' recaps. I don't want to be in your whatever-it-is school paper, so just beat it, you hear!"

"I would, honest, but this is important." Emma raised her voice to be heard. "This may change my life! And it's not for some report, and it's not even about you."

"Why are you here, if it's not about me?" Karyl demanded, her voice still taut with resentment and decades-old anger. "I lost four years of my life, you know that? Prison is no piece of cake, no matter what these law-and-order fanatics would have you believe. You let someone lock you into a tiny room!"

"I believe you," Emma agreed, sighing, wishing this woman would listen.

But Karyl just kept ranting. "And all the garbage in the newspapers—they said terrible things about me. I don't want to talk about that stuff. Can't you understand that?"

"It will only take a few minutes. I'm trying to find Leigh River Greenleaf," Emma explained.

Karyl's spate of words stopped abruptly. She blinked, as if seeing Emma for the first time. "That's why you looked familiar," she said, her voice dropping almost to a whisper. "Good God, no wonder—"

She stopped, and Emma felt her stomach knot with anxiety. "What? What do you know?"

Behind her, the bell on the door tinkled, and another customer came into the shop. Emma was forced to stand, shifting her weight from one foot to another, waiting for the woman to collect her clothes, crinkling in their plastic garment bag. Then a man entered with an armload of shirts. Emma felt her face flush with impatience. She had to talk to Karyl.

Surprisingly, Karyl also seemed annoyed at the interruptions. After the man had left his cleaning, she looked across at Emma, only to be interrupted yet again by the door's jingle.

"Harry, get out here," she yelled toward the back.

Apparently, she wasn't alone in the shop, after all. In a moment, a pimply-faced young man poked his head through the inner door. "What?"

"Come out here. I need to take a break."

"It's not time for me to take the counter," he complained. "I got a load of laundry that needs to come out."

"It can wait," Karyl insisted. "I gotta pee, for crying out loud. Get your butt out here."

He shrugged and came up to the counter to take care of the customer.

Karyl motioned to Emma, who hurried up to the side of the counter. "Come round to the alley door," the woman said, her voice low. Emma nodded, and Karyl vanished through the doorway into the nether regions of the laundry.

Emma left the shop, finding a narrow alley to the side of the building. She hoped this was not just another way for Karyl to get out of her sight; maybe it was a ruse. Or maybe the woman was dangerous, and meeting her out of public sight was not a good idea, either.

But Karyl knew something, Emma was sure of it, and she had to know the truth about Leigh, about the shadow twin who had haunted her life since the day Emma had seen the first photograph.

Her heart beating faster with anticipation, Emma picked her way carefully along the littered alley until she found a nondescript door at the side of the building. It wasn't labeled, but this was the same building, and surely this cracked stucco wall enclosed the rear of the dry cleaners. Emma stepped up to the door and knocked timidly.

For a moment, nothing happened, and Emma wondered if her first fear had been the right one. Karyl was not going to answer, not going to talk to her after all. Then the door opened with a creak of rusty hinges, and Karyl stood in the doorway.

"Come in," she said.

Emma gulped, feeling like the fly that the spider had invited to tea, but she stepped over the threshold into a crowded back room, hung with clothes in plastic casings and with sacks of—apparently—dirty laundry piled along one side. The air was thick with smells of chemicals and steam. At the other side of the room, a small table held a coffeemaker, paper cups, and packets of sugar and creamer. The beige tabletop was dotted with coffee stains and sugar and cookie crumbs.

Karyl poured herself a cup of strong black coffee; steam rose from the paper cup. She took one of the metal chairs and motioned to Emma to take the other.

"Want some coffee?" At least the woman's tone sounded a little friendlier.

Emma hesitated, then shook her head. Her stomach was already roiling with tension. She sat down on the rickety chair and waited.

"How the hell did you find me, anyhow?" Karyl asked, stirring her coffee and waiting for it to cool.

"I saw a poster of Leigh in the post office," Emma said. Karyl winced. "It had a street address on it. And when I saw the name of the dry cleaners, well, I remembered your name from the newspaper reports, Karyl Meadowlark Johansson."

Karyl shook her head, her expression wry. "Meadowlark. We were such fools; we were going to save the world, you know."

"That's not foolish," Emma argued, trying to find some way to connect with this strange woman. "Helping to save the environment is a great ambition."

"Yeah, well, it got me four years in a minimum security facility," Karyl muttered, taking a cautious sip.

"It's—it's just that the way you go about it matters, I guess," Emma said, then wished she'd bitten back the words.

As she'd feared, Karyl frowned again and set her coffee down too quickly; the dark liquid sloshed over the side of the cup.

"I didn't know nothing about that bank robbery! You think I wanted to kill some poor slob with kids at home? Even if he was a cop . . . I told them over and over I didn't know, but nobody would listen. They just wanted someone to blame. Tony was dead, and Leigh was missing, and they had to have someone to crucify. So poor old Tonya and me, we lost the crapshoot—too poor for decent lawyers, no rich loving family to bail us out. So much for saving the world." Her voice sank back to normal levels, and Karyl took a deep breath.

"But you must have had family who cared about you?" Emma asked, feeling a moment of pity she didn't dare express. "I mean, you came back to work in the family business, right?"

Karyl shrugged. "I'd always fought with my old man— he said I should stay home and do an honest day's work, not march around like a lunatic shouting about things I couldn't change. But he died while I was in prison, and I thought— well, I remembered how he'd looked in court at my trial, so tired, his shoulders slumped, his eyes red like he might have cried—I never saw him cry. And I wished I had tried to talk to him one last time . . ." She took a hasty sip of her coffee, her lids veiling her eyes, then added, "So when I got out, I came back to help my mom—she's got a heart condition, you know."

Emma didn't know, but she nodded and waited a moment, letting the hum of the machines from the other side of the wall fill the silence. Then she asked, very softly, "Did you know Leigh well?"

"Naw, I didn't know none of them that much. It was just a group I found when I was sort of lost and angry, and it seemed like a good idea, you know, making the world better, saving the forests, shutting down the nuclear power plants—enough poison in this world already." She sighed, looking around the shop. "My dad always said, 'Somebody had to make power and clean clothes.' "

Emma pushed back her wave of disappointment. "So Leigh wasn't from this neighborhood, after all?"

"I didn't say that." Karyl pulled a pack of cigarettes out of her sweater pocket and fished inside it once more for a box of matches. She took out one match and struck it, and the flame flared, then held it to her lips to light the cigarette.

Emma wrinkled her nose. No one smoked in her family, and she hated the sour smell, but this was not the time to complain. "So you did know her?"

"Oh, she lived down the street somewhere; we weren't best friends or anything. But yeah, she was the reason I hooked up with the group in the first place. She had this way of talking real gentle, her eyes so clear—that's the only thing different about you, you know, you don't have the same color eyes. Yours are too greenish. How the hell do you look so much like her, anyhow?"

"I don't know," Emma confessed. "That's one thing I'm trying to find out. I thought she might be a distant relative."

Karyl gazed at her over the cigarette. "Distant, huh. You look like her twin."

That part, Emma already knew. "Did Leigh have a big family? Brothers and sisters, maybe?"

"Not that I knew of." The other woman took the cigarette from her mouth and sipped her coffee again. "Just her dad, and he was no great piece of work."

"What do you mean?"

"A drunk, a mean drunk," Karyl said succinctly. "Beat her up a lot. She stayed at my place a few times to hide out from him. He broke her jaw once, knocked out a few teeth."

Emma felt a flicker of sympathy for her shadow self and pressed her lips together, as if feeling a vicarious pain. "What about her mom?"

"Dead, I think, long time ago." Karyl puffed on the cigarette.

Emma tried not to wince when the noxious smoke drifted her way. "Did you see Leigh again after—after the bank robbery and the explosion?"

Karyl gazed at the cracked plaster wall behind Emma's

head as if thinking deeply, her eyes unfocused, then she dropped her gaze to Emma and shook her head. "No, never. I thought maybe she was dead."

Emma had considered the same possibility. Had she come all this way only to have the trail fade away in this maddeningly inconclusive way?

"That's all I know," Karyl told her, as if thinking much the same. "So don't go bringing my name into it, okay?"

"I won't," Emma promised. "Anyhow, it's just for me—it's not like I'm going to tell the newspapers. And why would they care?"

Karyl shrugged. "We were pretty famous for a while, you know, even had our pictures in *Newsweek*." She took another pull on her cigarette, sounding almost proud of her moment of infamy.

Emma looked at her. "Really? Do you still have the photos?"

"Naw, I threw that stuff away a long time ago," Karyl said quickly. "The last time the police came to ask me—those dumb Feds, they never forget a case. She's dead, I told them, let it go."

Emma wished she could have seen the photos and accompanying story; maybe she could find it at the library, she told herself. She hadn't checked any of the news magazines, only newspaper accounts.

"What about the group itself? Is it still around?"

"I dunno. The arrests sort of damped the enthusiasm, you know? They had a little newsletter for a while—"

"A newsletter? What was the name?" Emma asked quickly.

"*Green Power.* But I think it may have folded, too, just like the protests."

"Karyl," a man's voice called from the front of the dry cleaners. "Come and take the counter."

"Keep your shirt on; I'm coming!" Karyl yelled in answer. She pushed her chair back and stood, looking at Emma, who took the obvious hint.

"Thanks for talking to me," she said. She took a slip of paper from her backpack. She had written her dorm address and phone on it. "If you think of anything else—"

"I won't," Karyl told her quickly. "And don't call me here. That's all over, I told you. I don't remember anymore."

Emma turned toward the door, then looked back over her shoulder for an instant. "I don't guess—Leigh never had a baby—did she?"

Karyl blinked and for an instant didn't meet Emma's gaze. "No, no, not that I knew of."

"Right." Emma headed for the doorway, feeling strangely blind for a moment as she walked into the light, then found herself outside in the alley again. She heard the door shut firmly behind her.

The woman had sounded truthful, Emma thought, most of the time. But that last statement had been a lie, Emma would swear to it. She walked slowly back to the street and headed for the bus stop.

Had there been a baby?

Was it possible that Emma was adopted?

Chapter
Twelve

Afterward, Emma didn't even remember how she'd gotten back to the dorm room. Obviously, she'd taken the right bus when it appeared, climbed on, and paid her fare; she had stepped off when she reached her Westwood stop and walked back to the campus and the residence hall. But she didn't remember one step, not one mile.

It seemed that one moment she was walking down Juniper Street in a daze, and the next that she was sitting on her bed in the small dorm room, fingering the scratchy blanket beneath her.

She was relieved that Sophie wasn't in the room; she must be out with classmates again. It was Friday, after all, and outside the sky was fading into a Technicolor sunset. Emma—when she pushed her blank mind into some semblance of action—vaguely recalled hearing Sophie mention this morning a local play many of the classmates were going to see.

Emma should have felt left out, lonely, but instead she

was grateful for the silence, the solitude of the empty room. She didn't want anyone else to see her like this, so dazed and shocked and almost panic-stricken. She felt as if her very foundation had been shaken. She didn't even know who she was anymore.

If she wasn't Emma Leigh Carter, daughter of Russell and Elizabeth, who was she? Had her whole life been a fraud? Had everything she knew—thought she knew about herself—been a lie? The thoughts made her physically sick; her stomach was roiling again, and she felt a dull pain around the top of her head, like a steel band that tightened inexorably.

Was it possible that Emma had been adopted, that Leigh River Greenleaf was her birth mother? That would explain the uncanny resemblance between them, from the long straight fair hair to the pale skin, the bump on the otherwise nicely proportioned nose, the tall slim frame, even perhaps their shared interest in the environment.

But why wouldn't her parents have told her? They were not old-fashioned, had never been close-minded about anything else. They had both talked to her about sex and responsibility early on. They had always exposed her to other cultures and taught her to accept different races and religions. If they could be enlightened in other ways, why on earth would they try to hide an adoption?

It made no sense. Emma drew a deep breath and tried to think calmly. If it didn't make sense, maybe it wasn't true. Her panic faded, and she thought of all the reasons why she couldn't be adopted. She and her brothers were all fair-haired, like her mom, before strands of gray had obscured her natural color. Her father's hair was an indeterminate sandy color, but he had been blond as a kid. Her brothers had her dad's hazel eyes, while Emma's were a peculiar greenish-blue, but that was not conclusive. She was fair-skinned, like both her parents, and tall, again like both of them. Her parents loved her, and they would not have perpetuated such an enormous lie. Surely, she was the person she had always thought she must be.

But the strange resemblance between Emma and Leigh River Greenleaf—how could she explain it? Emma thought vaguely of sperm banks, but that was for fathering children—it wouldn't affect who your mother was. As for the other side of the parenting equation . . . Nowadays some women donated eggs for other women having trouble conceiving—she remembered a discussion in her biology class at school—but Emma thought that technique was more recent. It wouldn't have happened eighteen or twenty years ago, she was pretty sure.

And it all left—what? She was back where she had started. Why did everything in this strange pilgrimage seem to lead nowhere? She found only confusing answers that doubled back on themselves or led to more questions. As a detective, she was lousy, Emma thought glumly. And she was sick of it.

The silence in the room seemed suddenly heavy, empty, and she was no longer glad to be alone. She wanted to hear voices, laughter, arguments no more serious than which was the greatest movie of all time, which her classmates debated endlessly. She wanted to be a teenager on a summer trip, a normal kid with no worries about who she was and what ghost lurked in her past. She wanted to forget it all and be happy again.

So when Sophie came home after midnight, Emma lay sprawled across the bed, trying to lose herself in an entertainment magazine she had found on top of the desk.

"Hi, was the play good?"

"Not bad, though the second act needed some work, and the climax was a bit flat," her roommate said. "You should have come with us."

"I know, I wish I had."

"Luke would have been happy if you did," Sophie told her, her dark eyes mischievous.

Emma shrugged, trying not to show that the remark pleased her. "I have a boyfriend at home."

"So? Homeboy's going off to college. Don't hurt to hedge your bets, girlfriend." Sophie winked. "You got a postcard in the mail today, did you see it? I picked it up for you when I got my mail."

Emma hadn't noticed the small card tucked into the edge of the mirror. Was it from Jay? She hurried to pull it out; the outer side had a picture of two old ladies at a beach, sitting primly under a frilly umbrella. She flipped it over and read:

> *Hey, best friend, hope you're having fun. I'm on my way to Florida tomorrow, so will be soaking up the rays, too, by the time you get this.*
>
> *Revi*
>
> *P.S. Heard Jay was seen at the movies with that Columbia freshman from down the street who's home for the summer. She's blonde and pretty, too. Guess he's taking this noncommitment thing seriously.* So have fun out in L.A.!

Emma bit her lip, feeling a wave of chagrin. Yes, they had agreed not to feel committed, but Jay hadn't wasted any time about it. She glanced back at Sophie.

"Read it, huh?"

Sophie shrugged. "Hey, it's a postcard—it just happened to catch my eye."

"Uh-huh," Emma said dryly. She tossed the card back onto her bed.

"We're going to the beach tomorrow. Why don't you stop all this extra work and come with us?" Sophie shed her clothes and pulled on an oversized sleep tee.

"I'd like that," Emma said firmly. Revi was right. Like Jay, she could have a free heart, too.

When Sophie turned out the light, Emma pulled the sheet up to her chin. Sleep was hard to grasp, and when she at last closed her eyes, she dreamed again, dreamed of fire and loud noises and fear—terrible fear. She woke sweating, twisted in her sheets, not sure for a moment where she was—or who she was.

Then the darkness settled over her like a blanket. Emma remembered: She was in a dorm room at UCLA, of course, and she was herself, she was, she was. She took long slow breaths to calm herself. Across the room she heard Sophie's measured, untroubled breathing, and outside, traffic noises drifted past the blinds.

Her body gradually relaxed, and Emma shut her eyes, trying not to fear the visions that might still linger. But this time she slept more normally, and when she opened her eyes again, daylight splashed the walls of their tiny room, and Sophie was already dressed.

"Get up, girl," Sophie called, her voice merry. "Got to get to the beach while there's still a spot left for us to sit."

Emma was happy to push herself out of bed and leave the nightmares behind. She dressed quickly in shorts and T-shirt, putting her swimsuit and towel into her backpack, then they met the rest of their group.

Luke grinned when he saw her. "Hi," he said, moving closer. "I'm glad you came."

"Me, too," Emma admitted, trying not to admit how much it pleased her to see the sparkle of admiration in his eyes.

"How was the play last night?" She listened to his critique as they walked across the street to a coffee shop for muffins and latte, then, carrying their breakfast, headed for the bus stop.

Emma sipped her milky coffee and ate her muffin during the bus ride, and when they arrived at the beach, found it much more crowded on the weekend. The sky was still misty with early-morning haze, but already the sand was littered with family groups, teens with boom boxes blaring, and even a homeless man dozing beneath a tattered blanket.

They eventually found an empty space on the sand big enough for all six of them to spread out their towels. Emma and Sophie and Kizzy walked up to the women's showers to change their clothes, then came back to drop their bags on the sand and hurry into the water. Hints of sunlight burned through the haze, and the air was warming.

"Come on," Luke said. "Let's see if you remember what I taught you about body surfing."

To Emma's pleasure, it was easier to fall into the pattern that Luke had showed her last time, flattening her body and letting the waves carry her into shore. She loved the sparkle of sunlight on the moving waves, the cries of seagulls overhead, the briny smell of the ocean, and most of all, the buoyant feeling that came with lying in the salty water.

Right now, there was nothing she wanted more than to feel free, light, released from all the worry and fear and uncertainty that had plagued her for weeks. She took a long ride in, with Luke a few feet away swept in on the same rushing wave, laughing in glee when she was close enough to put her feet down and touch the sand, then coughing when she accidentally swallowed some of the brackish water.

Luke pounded her on the back. "Okay?"

Emma nodded, but her eyes were watering, and she couldn't speak.

"Let's sit down for a few minutes," Luke suggested.

She followed him back to their towels. Sitting down, Emma searched through her bag to find a tissue and wiped her eyes and nose. "Wow," she said. "I tried to swallow it all that time."

Luke grinned as she found her water bottle inside her backpack and took a long drink. The scratchiness in her throat eased, and she lay back against the sand.

"Are you okay, Emma?" Luke asked.

"Yeah, I'm fine, now," Emma told him.

"No, I mean, really okay." Luke reclined on the hard-packed sand, one arm crooked beneath him to support his head as he regarded her intently.

Emma found herself flushing. "What do you mean?"

"Ever since you got here, it's like—like you've had something on your mind, something that worries you," Luke said.

Were all writers this observant? In some corner of her mind, Emma thought that Jay would never have noticed her distraction. Yet this guy she had just met seemed to sense her anxiety. "I—I just—"

"You don't have to tell me," Luke said, his voice quiet, "if you don't want to. But when you're always going off to 'work' instead of to the beach or out at night with the rest of us . . . I mean, I know the instructor isn't giving us that much homework. I just wondered if you were in some kind of trouble."

Emma shook her head. "One reason I haven't always gone out is that I—I have a boyfriend at home," she said, glancing down at the sand.

There was a short silence, then Luke said, "I should have known that. It's serious, then?"

Emma glanced at him quickly, his expression was unrevealing. "Not for sure. He's going off to college soon, and we've already agreed there's no commitment, that we're free to date other people."

"Oh," Luke murmured, but she sensed him relax a little.

"But you're right; there's more. I came out here hoping

to find out something about a woman whose photograph I saw—a woman who, almost twenty years ago—looked just like me."

Emma told him, in a few words, the gist of what had happened, and ended with, "Now I'm wondering if I'm adopted. But why wouldn't my parents had told me? It's not like them. They've always been honest with me."

"Maybe they were afraid of losing you, somehow. Maybe there's something you don't know," Luke told her.

It had pleased her that he seemed to take her concerns seriously. He had not suggested that she was paranoid, crazy for dreaming up these far-fetched scenarios. He was a writer, after all. But she felt a flicker of fear when he seemed to agree that her newest worry might be a real possibility.

"I don't think so," she said, hearing the stubbornness in her tone. "I don't think they would lie to me like that."

"Then what do you think is the answer?" Luke asked reasonably.

Emma sighed. "That's the problem; I don't know. And every clue I find keeps leading me in circles. I'm ready to scream. And I have these terrible dreams."

Luke lifted his brows. "Anxiety dreams?"

"I guess," Emma said. "All these bits and pieces of the newspaper stories; you know how dreams are. But it doesn't help the way I feel."

"I guess not," Luke agreed. "I hope you find the answers you want, Emma, answers you can live with."

She shivered. "Me, too," she said, rubbing absently at her shoulder, which felt tender.

"You're turning pink," Luke observed.

"Oh, I forgot to put on sunscreen." Emma frowned at her own forgetfulness. "I'll look like a lobster." She dug into her backpack and found the sunscreen, squeezing out handfuls and rubbing it on her legs and arms.

"Here, I'll do your back," Luke offered.

Emma rolled onto her stomach and relaxed against the beach towel as Luke stroked the sunscreen over her shoulders and back. The slow, easy movements of his hand sent waves of warmth through her that seemed to reach all the way to her bones, a heat that the sun-warmed cream had nothing to do with. His touch on her bare skin . . . yes, there were certainly sparks between them, as Sophie had observed. Even though he lacked the dramatic good looks of her high school sweetheart, Luke's blue-gray eyes and strong rugged features grew more appealing the longer she knew him.

But Luke was going to UCLA in the fall, and in a year she was almost certainly going to college in the East. At least she was if she listened to her mom.

Emma wondered idly if she could ever talk her mom into a West Coast university, instead. It was wonderful to concentrate on such a mundane kind of concern, instead of the life-shaking anxieties she had been wrestling with for days.

She no longer felt guilty about Jay—she had told Luke about him and as Revi had pointed out, Jay was already ranging freely.

Still, it was way too soon to think about other romances. For one thing, by the time she went off to college, Luke would likely have found another girlfriend. But she could enjoy today. Feeling Luke's hands sliding smoothly over her back, Emma relaxed and forgot to be afraid.

She dozed a while on the sand, then they went back into the water, and then joined Sophie and the others for a lively game of Frisbee. Hunger eventually sent them to one of the snack bars that bordered the beach, and they walked back to their towels laden with sandwiches and soft drinks.

When the sun lay heavy on the watery horizon, Emma and the other girls headed for the small block building to stand in line to shower off the saltwater and change into their clothes. Then it was time to pack everything up and head for the bus stop. Emma felt pleasantly tired as her sandals slid through the softer sand before they reached the pavement. Today she had thought only of good things, she told herself, and she wanted more days like this. She had to shake the shadow that had hung over her since she'd found the newspaper photos; she had to get her life back.

"Want to try a movie tonight?" Luke asked as they boarded the bus.

She glanced at him, and he added quickly, "Everyone is going, and this new director is supposed to be really hot. *Variety* says he's the new Spike Lee."

Emma grinned. "Sure."

So after a quick stop at the dorm to leave her bag and put on a little makeup, she and Sophie met the rest of the group and walked to a large cinema complex where she sat next to Luke, and even toward the end of the movie rested her head lightly against his shoulder. It had a good solid feel, and she shut her eyes for a moment against the flickering images on the screen. This was good.

When the movie ended, they walked back to the campus, discussing the movie. Emma found herself yawning.

"Sorry," she said, abashed that she had yawned into one of Luke's observations about the director's style.

He grinned. "The beach will do that to you," he said. He didn't sound offended, and Emma—who had wondered earlier if he would want to kiss her when they said good night—relaxed. The truth was, she would have been happy to kiss Luke, but better not to rush it, she told herself.

"See you tomorrow," he said, grinning as if he could follow her thoughts.

Nodding, she waved, and then followed Sophie into the women's residence. Long-distance relationships were hard to maintain—everyone knew that. But she couldn't help liking Luke, liking the firm curve of his jaw and the intelligent gleam in his eyes, the way that he really listened to her when she spoke, the way he noticed how she felt, even when she tried to hide her worries. Having Luke in her life would be a good thing, Emma thought.

" 'Bout time you came out of your cocoon," Sophie told her.

Emma grinned. "Yeah, I'm glad I came today."

"And you're going with us tomorrow," Sophie said firmly. "Boy, being in the water makes me hollow down to my toes." Sophie picked up the paper bag left over from Emma's trip to the bakery and rummaged inside for a cookie. "You need to go back to Juniper Street. They got tasty stuff."

"What?" Emma felt a sudden shock, as if she'd accidentally trod on a live wire. "What did you say?"

"I said, the bakery has mucho tasty—"

"No, the name of the street, say it again," Emma said, feeling somehow breathless. "You said, Who—something."

"Juniper?"

Her Hispanic roommate, a native Angelino, was giving Juniper the Spanish pronunciation, Emma realized, where the *J* sounded like a *wh.*

All this time, Emma had been thinking of a *J* as in *Jupiter* or *Jake,* and she'd never actually heard anyone pronounce the name of the street.

"So? What's the matter, Emma?" Sophie's puzzled voice sounded far away.

Emma was inside her head, listening to an old, old memory, hearing her mother's voice saying, "It was a small bakery on Juniper Street where I grew up with my grandmother . . ."

Now that she knew what the street was accurately

called, now that she heard it, the name had triggered the memory. It was not just some random street in a rundown part of Los Angeles, it was a name from her past—but what did it mean?

Chapter
Thirteen

"Emma? What's wrong?" Sophie demanded, coming over to shake her lightly. "You're white as my mama's best sheets, girl."

"I—I just got a really bad headache," Emma managed to say, rubbing her temple, which was indeed aching with a piercing pain.

"You must've been out in the sun too long," Sophie said, shaking her head. "Lie down. Need an aspirin? Want me to get you a cold cloth for your head?"

"Thanks, a cold cloth would be great," Emma agreed. She almost fell into her narrow bed and lay with her eyes shut until Sophie brought a damp cloth from the bathroom. Then Emma put it over her forehead and lay silently as Sophie clicked off the lights. Emma's thoughts were a whirl of confusion; she felt as if she had plunged into the whirling heart of a tornado.

Her mother—her mother was connected to Juniper Street. Not just the unknown and mysterious Leigh River Greenleaf, nor the recalcitrant Karyl Johansson, but her very own mild-mannered, charity-chairperson, benefit-giving, staid, prematurely gray mother. It made no sense at all.

But her mother was from California originally, Emma knew that. And her dad had gone to medical school at UCLA—that was where the two had met and later married. Was it possible that—that her mom had known Leigh, too, as a girl? Did that mean that the adoption was a possibility—maybe her mother and dad had taken a baby that the radical protester couldn't care for. It wouldn't surprise Emma about her mom or her dad to imagine them taking in an infant who needed help—but to never tell her . . . Why would they do that?

Oh, God, what was she going to do? She had to find out the truth. She wanted to pick up the phone and call her parents, demand to know if adoption was the answer.

But across the room, Sophie turned in her bed, obviously still awake, and Emma wasn't ready to blurt out all her questions in front of such a new friend, nice as her roommate had been.

Instead, she lay back against the sheets, feeling her stomach churn with unresolved mysteries. For a long time she lay there, staring into the darkness, feeling as shaken as if the earth had moved beneath her. One of the famous California earthquakes could not have unsettled her more. Every new fact she discovered led only to more questions, more uncertainty, more anxiety that threatened the foundations of her world.

Where would it all end? In the blackness of the longest night she had ever known, listening to the drone of traffic noise outside her window, Emma wondered if she had the courage to see this pilgrimage through to its end—whatever that might be . . .

Somewhere toward dawn, she slept at last, dreaming confused snatches of nightmarish visions that she could not remember when she awoke. Somehow, she was a baby, and she was hiding her head against her pillow, while in another room, someone sobbed . . .

When Emma managed to fight her way through the heavy layers of sleep, blinking in confusion against the sunlight that warmed the room, she heard the shower running and saw that Sophie's bed was already empty. For a moment Emma lay still, trying to remember why she felt so heavy and tired, then she sat up suddenly, remembering her difficult night and the newest questions that had emerged from her hazy memory of her mother's comment about Juniper Street.

Pushing aside the covers, Emma ran for the phone. Stopping to grab her purse and find her phone card, she dialed the number and waited impatiently for the phone to ring. When at last it did, Emma held her breath, picturing the phone in the hall ringing and her little dog, Happy, running up and down, barking as he waited for someone to end the annoying noise.

But when the ringing stopped, it was the recorded voice on the answering machine that she heard. "You have reached the Carter residence; please leave a message at the beep."

Emma swallowed hard, and then slowly set the phone back into its base. She didn't want to leave a message about the most important question she might ever have in her life. What if one of her little brothers picked up the message? How could she explain it?

She felt bitterly disappointed, wishing she had not slept so late. Her father had probably gotten up early to make his hospital rounds, then met her mom and brothers for late service at church, and then taken them out to lunch in a nice restaurant. One of his partners must be on call this weekend, and her dad would take advantage of the free time.

Picturing the scene, her brothers squabbling quietly, careful not to irk their parents too much, her mother smiling across the table at her dad, her dad perusing the menu and then looking up to return the smile, patting his wife's hand—Emma felt a wave of homesickness so painful that it made her swallow hard.

She wanted to be with them, sitting at the table between her brothers to keep the boys from jabbing each other with their salad forks; she wanted to scan the menu and pick out her own lunch while she watched the quiet contentment that flowed between her parents, to enjoy the love that kept her whole family centered and strong, a love so calm and deep she hardly ever thought about it.

Why was she so far away, in a strange city on the other side of the country? She might as well be on Mars. She wished she had never come, never learned all these disturbing facts—or guesses—about the girl in the newspaper photos who might or might not be connected to Emma, but who had certainly managed to destroy all her peace of mind.

Lost in a fog of self-pity, Emma didn't hear her roommate come back into the room until Sophie spoke.

"You look like you been sentenced to do hard time, instead of having a day at the beach in front of you," Sophie teased.

"Oh," Emma said. "Right." She picked up a towel and headed for the shower, trying to think how she would explain to Sophie that she couldn't face a day on the sand, not today. Yesterday's pleasant interlude with Luke beside her already seemed as if it had happened years ago. She had hoped to escape her private doubts, but the fear had all returned, twice as strong.

The hot water splashed her face as she shampooed her hair. She finished her shower quickly, then wrapped her long hair in a towel as she dressed. When she came back into the bedroom, Sophie was picking up her backpack.

"I'll wait for you outside," her roommate said. "The

others are meeting us at the corner. We'll get a muffin and then head for the bus stop."

"I can't go," Emma said flatly.

Sophie's eyes widened, and she stopped, letting her backpack slide off her shoulder. "Why not? Yesterday, you said—"

"I know, I'm sorry." Emma couldn't meet her friend's puzzled gaze. "Something came up—something I need to handle."

"Emma, are you in some kind of trouble? You're not into something stupid, are you? Tripping out on drugs, or—"

Emma shook her head. "No, of course not. I've never used drugs."

"Then why these sudden changes of mood; one minute you're happy, the next the world is ending, by the look on your face! I don't get it."

"I can't explain, I'm sorry. It's a family problem."

Sophie stared at her for a minute, then shrugged and lifted her backpack again. "You want to talk about it, I'll be glad to listen. Sure you don't want to come with us?"

Emma sighed. "No, but tell Luke I'm—I'm really sorry."

"Yeah, he will be, too," Sophie noted, her tone dry. She walked out the door and pulled it shut behind her.

Emma pulled a cotton sweater around her shoulders and picked up her own backpack. She paused to lock the door behind her, and when she turned, almost bumped into the tall boy who'd walked up behind her.

"Luke!" she exclaimed in surprise. "What are you doing here? I thought you were on your way to the beach with the others."

"I told them to go on without me," he said, his tone even, but his clear gray eyes serious. "What's wrong, Emma? Sophie said you looked totally out of it, but you won't tell her why. She's beginning to think you're suffering alien abductions, or something else just as weird."

Emma tried to laugh, but the sound was more like a groan. "I found out something else—"

"About the mystery girl?" Luke asked.

She nodded and explained about Juniper Street, and the memory evoked when she had heard the name.

"There's a connection between this girl and my mother, and maybe to me, but I don't know exactly what it is. But I can't just go off to the beach and relax when I don't know. I have to do something!"

"What?" Luke asked.

"I'm going back to the bakery, first of all," Emma told him. "I want to speak to the owner, find out if they know anything about my mother. Her grandmother owned a small bakery—it may not be the same one, but it was on the same street, and it's a place to start."

"Did you ask your mother?" Luke suggested. "That could save a lot of time."

Emma made a face. "I called home this morning, but no one's home. And it's Sunday—they might be out all day, at a museum or on a picnic in the park."

"And you can't bear to wait," Luke guessed, putting out one hand to lightly touch her cheek.

His touch was infinitely comforting, yet it also made her want to cry.

"Then let's go," Luke said. "We'll miss a bus while we stand here."

She looked at him in surprise. "But what about the beach?"

"It'll still be there tomorrow," he said with a shrug. "Right now, I think you need a friend."

Emma had to blink to hold back tears of relief. For the first time, she didn't feel so alone. And Luke—somehow, she trusted Luke. He wouldn't repeat her secrets, she was sure of it.

Nodding because she didn't trust her voice, they walked together into the hazy morning.

They stopped to buy Emma a muffin and a banana, only because Luke insisted. "You won't make much of a detective if you're faint from hunger," he told her, and then made their way to the bus stop to wait for the right number bus.

When it pulled up to the stop. they climbed on and paid their fares. On a Sunday, the bus was half empty, and they sat together in a front seat as the vehicle chugged its way across town.

While she ate the crumbly lemon-poppy muffin, Emma listened as Luke talked easily about their class—safe, non-threatening subjects that allowed her stomach to settle and the knot of tension inside her to ease.

Emma peeled the banana and gave Luke half. When she was done, she wiped her hands on the napkin before looking around for a trash container. She saw none, so she stuffed the banana peel and napkin into her pocket until she could find a garbage can. She couldn't just dump it on the bus. None of her mother's children would litter, she thought ruefully, not even her little brothers. Her mom had been into conservation before it became fashionable. Did that, too, date back to her childhood in California?

When they reached Juniper Street, they got off the bus and walked along the street until they reached the bakery. It was open—she hadn't thought to wonder if it would be, on a Sunday—and several customers were perusing the glass cases full of baked goods.

Luke pulled open the door, and the two of them walked into smells of sweet pastry. They lingered in front of the long clear shelves, looking over tall cakes heavy with chocolate icing, fruit-dotted flans, and cream-topped éclairs. Normally, the pastry would have made Emma's mouth water, but today she was too nervous to think about eating.

She waited impatiently for the rest of the people to be served, and when their turn came, she walked across to the middle-aged woman with the Asian face who waited behind the counter.

"Can I help you?" The woman had a slight accent, but her smile was friendly.

"I'd like to speak to the owner, please," Emma said politely.

"I am the owner. You got a problem?" The woman's eyes narrowed, and her smile faded.

"No, no. I bought some cookies and tarts the other day and they were wonderful," Emma said honestly. "I just want to ask you some questions."

"What about?" The woman still sounded suspicious.

"I'm trying to track down some distant relatives," Emma said, trying to stick to the truth as much as possible. "Do you know anyone named Leigh Grimble?"

The woman shook her head, her expression perplexed.

"Any Grimble at all?"

"No." The bakery owner picked up a white cloth and wiped up a crumb. "Listen, I got work—"

"My mother lived on Juniper Street when she was small, and her grandmother owned a bakery, a small one, like this. But it burned down when my mother was a teenager—over two decades ago. Do you know where that might be? It's probably built over by now, and there may be another building where it once stood—"

The woman frowned. "I don't know any other bakery on this end of Juniper 'cept ours, and it been here forty years—more, maybe. I been here thirty years, and I don't remember any fire. I think you got the wrong address, missy."

She turned and walked away.

Swallowing her frustration, Emma looked at Luke.

"A real mystery," he muttered. He reached for her hand.

She was glad to feel the warmth of his skin, the firm pressure as his fingers gripped hers.

"Maybe you do have the wrong place."

"Maybe," she admitted, "but I know it was Juniper Street in my mother's story."

"But you said there are several Junipers on the map."

"I know." Luke held the door for her, and they stepped out onto the pavement, noisy with the rumble of passing cars and vans, the smell of exhaust in the smoggy air, and all around them, the clatter of people talking and music blaring. Even on Sunday, Los Angeles hummed with life.

"This way," she told him and hurried down the street to the dry cleaning shop where Karyl Johansson worked. But when they reached it, the door was firmly locked and the sign on the glass read, CLOSED.

Now what? Emma thought about tracking down all the Junipers listed on the city map, walking each foot of pavement, asking countless questions and finding only more dead-ends. She sighed.

"I could go back to the newspaper archives," she said, thinking aloud. "And look for fires about the right time that my mom's bakery burned. But I don't know the date, exactly."

"And a city this size must have an awful lot of fires," Luke noted. "You're sure there was a fire?"

When she turned to glare at him, he added, "I mean, you said you were little when you heard the story, maybe you misunderstood about the bakery being destroyed. Maybe it was only a small blaze, and afterwards, your mom's family sold the bakery."

Emma shook her head. "No, I'm sure. Anyhow, my mother still has burn scars on the side of her face, even after plastic surgery. There must have been a fire."

Luke nodded. Relaxing for a moment, Emma leaned against him; he felt solid and strong and infinitely reassuring. He just had to believe her, had to be on her side. She didn't think she could keep going all alone. It was too hard.

"What can I do now?" Wait till tomorrow and call her mother and demand more details, Emma thought. But she couldn't bear to wait a whole day and do nothing.

"Have you tried looking up this Leigh person's birth certificate?" Luke asked.

"Can you do that?" Emma turned to him quickly, excited by this new idea.

"I think so," Luke said. "I don't know how, exactly, but we can find out."

Cheered, Emma gave him a quick hug.

Luke laughed. "I'll have to come up with more brainstorms," he said, his voice teasing. "Maybe the next one will rate a kiss, too."

They took the bus back to Westwood and stopped at the nearest branch of the public library, but it, too, was closed on Sunday.

Emma stared at the sign, affronted.

Luke shrugged. "We'll have to go to the university library, that's all."

"Of course." She wasn't thinking straight; the unending stress was getting to her, Emma thought. She wanted to find the answers and get back to her life, reclaim her world and forget about Leigh and her difficult life and—perhaps—untimely death.

As they walked back to the campus, she shared that theory with Luke. "What if she's dead? The newspaper accounts just faded away."

"You could check for death certificates, too," Luke said.

"That will only work if someone knew she was dead," Emma told him, frowning at the thought. "If she were hurt, too, in the explosion—"

"Explosion?" Luke's brows lifted.

She explained about the bank robbery attempt and the resulting explosion as they approached the library desk.

After showing their temporary student IDs, they were directed to the right department.

Soon they were both scrunched into chairs in front of the same computer and, following the librarian's direction, had found the Web site for the Los Angeles County Register.

As they leaned forward to read the directions, Emma rested her head for a moment against Luke's shoulder—she was so glad he was here. But what she read on the computer screen jerked her upright again in alarm.

"Twenty days! I don't want to wait twenty days for an answer, for crying out loud!"

"Here, look—if you have a credit card, you can pay for expedited service, only three days." Luke had read farther down the page. He scrolled the data on the computer screen, and Emma read the next paragraph, too.

"I have one of my mom's credit cards, I can do that," she agreed.

As Luke watched, she filled in the form for Leigh River Greenleaf, also known as Leigh Grimble, birth date unknown, address 574 Juniper Street, Los Angeles.

She added the credit card number and sent the form into cyberspace, breathing a sigh of hope.

Before they logged off, she had another thought. "I'm going to put in my mom's name," she said. "It might give me the street number of the bakery—they lived in an apartment over the shop. Maybe I could find out more about her family, and see—see if there's any chance that an adoption did take place."

She filled out another form with her mom's name and birth date, listing Juniper Street again, and sent it winging through cyberspace, too.

Then, feeling that she had accomplished something, Emma felt more hopeful than she had all week.

Luke rubbed her shoulders gently, and she felt some of her tension ease.

"Are you hungry?" he asked. "I'm starved. How about we get something to eat, and maybe go see a movie. You need a break."

Emma nodded. "Sounds great."

They walked out of the library side by side, and it seemed natural to take his hand. Emma's heart lifted, and for a while, she would push away the dark clouds that had threatened her for so long. They found a small Mexican restaurant, and Emma burned her tongue again with spicy and delicious food.

Then they walked to the large theater complex in Westwood and watched another movie, later stopping for an ice-cream sundae as they dissected the movie. This class had opened her eyes to so much about movie making; she would never think of any film as just a movie again, Emma thought.

And most of all, she had met Luke.

Chapter
Fourteen

Emma slept much better that night, without troubling dreams. She went to class on Monday, soothed by the thought that in two more days she would have the birth certificates, which would surely provide more clues.

When she woke, she considered calling her mother, but although she stared at the phone on the desk, she couldn't bring herself to pick it up.

What if Emma was wrong about the whole thing? Worse, what if she was right? Now that she knew that the birth certificates were coming, she wanted more answers before she confronted her mom. Because if there had been an adoption and she hadn't been told, Emma was going to be very, very angry. Better not to start the shouting until she was sure.

Ironically, the class discussion today was about classic mystery movies; the instructor discussed how to make a good mystery work.

"You need clues scattered carefully through the whole movie," he noted. "Subtle hints that won't be too obvious, but later, when the answers become known, the audience will say, 'Oh, yeah, I remember that, but I didn't quite pick up on it.' You have to tease the audience along, not give away too much too soon, but lay the groundwork for your final solution."

He turned on a movie clip to illustrate his point, and while the figures flickered on the screen, Emma's thoughts reverted to her own private mystery.

Were there clues that she was missing? The thought pulled at her; she could almost feel stray bits of information floating in the back of her mind. What had Karyl said—something Emma had meant to follow up on, but in the rush of subsequent events, she'd forgotten.

Emma frowned, trying to remember the details of the conversation she had had with the ex-activist in the back of the dry cleaning shop.

A newsletter! Karyl had said the environmental group had put out a newsletter. *Green* something—*Green Power.* Emma should check at the library and try to see if it still existed. It might help her find more of the original protestors. Would any of the group know where Leigh was today, or if she was still alive?

Emma hardly heard the rest of the class, sitting impatiently until the period ended. When the instructor released them, Emma grabbed her backpack and stood up quickly.

"Emma?" Sophie said from across the aisle. "You going to the beach with us today?"

Emma hesitated, and Sophie made a face. "Tell me you're not going to hide out in some library again, girl. It's a gorgeous day out there!"

If she didn't go, Luke might give up his trip to the beach, too. She felt guilty, because of Luke. He had stopped to say something to the instructor; Emma glanced toward the front of the room where they talked. "Just one thing I need to check," she said. "If you'll give me an hour, I'll be there, I promise."

Sophie threw up her hands in mock disgust. "You're nuts! Okay, we'll get some lunch before we leave. But if you're not at the bus stop in one hour sharp—"

"I will be, I promise," Emma said. She looked back at the front, where Luke still chatted with their teacher. "Tell Luke, okay? And if you don't mind, pick up my swimsuit and a towel when you go by the room to get your stuff."

"If it'll get you there on time, sure." Sophie rolled her eyes in mock despair.

Emma didn't wait any longer; she took off for the library at a run. Fortunately, the reference librarian knew how to find a list of past and current newsletters, and Emma sat down at a desk and scanned the pages of narrow type.

There were a lot of environmental newsletters, but she found *Green Power* quickly, and after closer scrutiny, Emma was pretty sure this had to be the right one. SAVE OUR PLANET NOW! The headline read in glaring letters; the angry mood seemed right for the militant extremist group she sought. After some searching, the librarian found a few copies of the newsletter on microfilm for her, but they were over ten years old.

Emma read them anyhow, glancing at her watch. She didn't have much time. She scanned the few sheets quickly; the pages were amateurish and filled with raging diatribes but not much real information. It was no wonder the newsletter had died. Emma saw few names mentioned, but she did write down the phone number listed on the newsletter, and the P.O. box number.

Then she had to return the microfilm and run for the bus stop. She'd had no time for lunch, but she'd get a snack at the beach.

The others were all there. Luke waved when he saw her. Panting, she ran up just as a bus pulled in, its brakes shrieking as the door wheezed open.

"Good timing," Luke said, reaching out a hand to half-pull her up the steps. "I was afraid you weren't going to make it."

She threw her arms around him, balancing on the step as they waited their turn to pay their fares. Any excuse, she could hear Revi saying in her mind, imagining her friend laughing. She couldn't wait to tell Revi about Luke, about how special he was.

The line moved forward, and they climbed the last step, bought their tickets, and pushed back through the line of people already standing in the middle of the bus. One of the nearby passengers reeked heavily of garlic; Emma wrinkled her nose and motioned to Luke to edge farther back. The vehicle moved forward with a jerk, and again, Emma found herself putting one arm around Luke's waist, to steady herself, she thought.

But the truth was, she loved the solid feel of him next to her. And he didn't seem to mind; grinning, he looked back at her, then half-turned so he could put one arm around her shoulders.

It was too noisy to try to talk—a boom box blared from the back, and around them, conversations rose in half a dozen languages. But Emma was content just to stand there, braced against the roll and sway of the bus, her hair blowing from the draft that flowed through an open window.

She felt more at ease now, sure that answers were coming with the birth certificates, and for a few days, she could forget her worries. When they reached the beach stop, she and Luke and Sophie and the other kids piled off the bus and walked the rest of the way, chatting easily about the film class that morning, about the size of the waves crashing against the beach. They spread out their towels on the firmly packed sand and soon had shed their clothes and changed into swimsuits, then headed for the water.

The sky was clear and blue, with only streaks of wispy clouds far overhead. Above them, seagulls circled in large flocks, and one brave bird zipped toward the sand and snatched a bread crust within inches of Emma's towel.

Laughing, she poured sunscreen on her palm and rubbed it into her skin. Luke came to massage the lotion onto her back, and she relished the feel of his strong fingers against her skin.

"Look." Luke pointed toward the horizon, and Emma squinted to see the flashing arc of sleek gray that rose above the waves.

"What is it?"

"Dolphin," he told her.

Fascinated, she watched the animal cavorting in the clear water until it swam farther out to sea and disappeared from view. For a moment, Emma thought of Revi, having contact up close with these fascinating creatures, and wished she could have been in Florida, too. But she wouldn't have met Luke in Florida; she'd take his company over dolphins and porpoises, intriguing as the animals were, any day.

They spent the rest of the afternoon in the water, body surfing and swimming, or playing on the beach with an inflatable ball that kept slipping away from them as gusts of wind snatched it out of reach. When they tired, they lounged on the sand, listening to reggae music from a neighboring group of kids a few feet away, who played their music loud enough for the whole beach to hear.

When at last they walked back to the bus stop, pleasantly tired and a little red from the wind and sun, Emma sighed happily. She'd like more days like this, unfettered by worry and nagging doubts.

"It's good to see you smile," Luke murmured into her ear as if he had been thinking much the same.

"It feels good," she said. "I'm glad I came."

The bus they rode back to Westwood was crowded with people getting off work, so again they had to stand. They stopped for dinner at a Chinese restaurant, and shared dishes of exotic, steamy food.

Ravenous from all the swimming and running, Emma ate until she felt she might explode. Sophie picked up a small plate of fortune cookies and passed it around.

"Test your fortune," she suggested, teasing.

Emma took one of the cookies, broke the hard cookie shell and read the fortune: "You will find your heart's desire," it read. She felt herself blush.

"What?" Sophie demanded. "Mine says, 'You are universally esteemed.' Phooey."

"I had the same," Emma lied, not quite looking at Luke. "What about yours?" she asked him.

"I'll tell you later," he said.

As they walked back to the dorm, they separated into smaller groups of twos and threes, and Emma found herself beside Luke, holding his hand. Ahead of them, Sophie and Kizzy went inside the building, but Emma paused on the steps to say good night to Luke.

"Now ask me what my fortune cookie said," he told her.

"Okay, what?" Emma answered obediently.

"It said, 'You will kiss a beautiful girl.'"

"You're making that up!"

"Hey, I'm a writer; I revise," he pointed out.

Before she could laugh, he leaned closer and touched her lips with his own. It was a soft, sweet, gentle kiss, and Emma had no wish to pull away.

The kiss lingered, grew stronger, and Emma leaned into his arms. When at last they pulled apart, Emma felt strangely breathless.

"Wow," she said softly.

"Double wow," he agreed, his gray eyes bright. "I better leave now while I still have an ounce of resolution left."

He squeezed her hand and strode away. She slipped inside the outer doors and walked slowly to her room.

Inside, Sophie was in her robe, a towel in her hand, but she grinned at the sight of her roommate.

"Who's been smooching on the front steps?"

"What, you were looking?" Emma stuck out her tongue.

"Didn't have to, girl. You got that 'just been kissed and kissed right' look about you."

Emma felt her face flush. "Get out of here."

Sophie laughed and headed for the shower.

It was true, Emma thought. Jay's kisses had never made her feel like this. She felt a twinge of guilt, and on impulse, sat down to dial Jay's number back in Oak Grove. Maybe she should tell him about Luke, tell him she'd met another boy . . .

But when the phone was answered, it was his mother's voice she heard.

"Oh, hello, Emma," Mrs. Lewkoski said. "I'm afraid Jay isn't here right now. I'll tell him you called." She sounded just a little self-conscious.

He's out with another girl, Emma thought. And she didn't care.

She said good-bye and broke the connection. She was about to hang up the phone when she remembered the phone number she had taken from the out-of-date newsletter at the library. Digging into her backpack, she found the slip of paper where she had scribbled the phone number, then picked up the phone.

It rang several times, then, to her disappointment, she heard a recorded voice say, "This number is no longer in service."

Drat. Emma hung up the phone slowly. Oh well, she had the birth certificates coming, she reminded herself. They would tell her something, give her a new direction to follow.

And today had been a wonderful day. Emma sighed happily and found a clean towel and her sleep tee, ready to wash off the saltwater and collapse into a dreamless sleep.

Or maybe, to dream about Luke, she thought, and more silken kisses . . .

The next two days were the happiest she had spent since coming to Los Angeles. She went to class, could actually concentrate on the lively discussions, and afterwards, she would hang out with Luke and the others, go to the beach, in the evening visit a rehearsal at a local theater and listen to the director's comments. And always, Luke was there, meeting her eye when something really funny happened, his gray eyes merry. She had begun to realize how much she was going to miss him when she returned home.

Only one thing happened to jar her newfound ease. On Tuesday she checked at the student post office; the birth certificates hadn't arrived, but there was a short note from her mom, which Emma read quickly—"Hope you're having a good time; we miss you," and another crumbled envelope with an L.A. postmark.

Emma ripped it open quickly. Inside was a much folded newspaper clipping, yellowed with age, and a short note.

Found this stuck in the back of a bureau drawer; it's all I have. I don't know nothing else.

Karyl

Emma unfolded the clipping; it was a photo of the protest group, one that Emma hadn't seen before. From the heading at the top, this picture had apparently been published in a smaller local paper. Karyl was in the foreground, holding a sign that read, STOP KILLING OUR WORLD! and beside her was Leigh River Greenleaf, or Leigh Grimble. The caption read only, "Local protestors disrupt city hall deliberations," without listing names, but Emma knew that fair hair and familiar face by now almost as well as her own, which it so eerily echoed. She stared at the photo.

Something in the angle of the blonde head sparked a half-buried memory, too, but she couldn't quite capture it.

Behind the girls stood a man, tall and long-haired, his face contorted as he struggled with a policeman. It was the man who had later died in the bomb explosion—Tony—the one who had tried to rob the bank.

Emma stared at the creased photo, trying to see past the faded black-and-white image into the minds of the protestors. At what point had they decided that they could break the law to save the world? Didn't they see the illogic in that reasoning? Sighing, she put the photo into her backpack, with the other copies she always carried with her, and went on to class.

Afterwards, when she went back to her dorm room, she looked up the number of the dry cleaning shop. A nasal-voiced man answered.

"Is Karyl there?" Emma asked.

"Hang on," he said. There was a silence, and she could hear the hum of machinery come across the open line.

Then a woman said "Hello?" into the phone, her voice cautious.

"It's me, Emma Carter," Emma said. "I just wanted to say thanks for sending the clipping. And if you find anything else—"

"I won't! And I told you not to call here," Karyl said, sounding agitated.

"I just—"

There was a click, and the connection was broken.

Emma frowned at the receiver, then replaced it slowly. What a strange person Karyl was—helpful one moment, rude and unpredictable the next.

Sighing, she grabbed her swimsuit and a towel and hurried to join the others. Luke would be waiting.

On Wednesday, Emma woke very early, her whole body tense. What? The room was quiet, and across the room, Sophie still breathed slowly, her eyes shut and her dark curly hair tangled on her pillow.

Then Emma remembered. This was it; today, she should receive the birth certificates. Today, maybe, she would find out the answers to some of the questions she had lived with for weeks.

Emma dressed quietly so as not to wake Sophie, then slipped out of the dorm room. When she checked her box, the mail hadn't yet been put out.

Gritting her teeth with impatience, Emma decided she would get a cup of coffee. But she had been in such a hurry, she hadn't even picked up her backpack, she realized, suddenly noticing the unaccustomed lightness, no weight dragging at her shoulder.

She dug into her jeans pockets and found a couple of dollar bills, enough for coffee, at least. She found a hot drink machine and punched the top button, watching the paper cup drop down into the slot and fill with dark liquid. Then she sipped the steaming, bitter brew and grimaced at the taste. Going outside, she walked up and down and drank the coffee, shivering a little in the early-morning haze.

Finally, checking her watch for the third time, she dumped the cup into the waste bin and hurried back to her box. This time, it held two official-looking envelopes. Emma pulled them out and ripped open the first one.

This was it! Leigh Anne Grimble, birth date, parents' names, and home address. And the street number was different: 489 Juniper Street this time; perhaps this building would still be standing.

Emma felt a surge of excitement. Armed with new information, perhaps now she would be able to find someone who knew—who remembered Leigh Grimble, who might know if she had had a baby. Come to think of it, Emma could check the birth records again, maybe, or were the birth certificates of babies given up for adoption handled differently? Maybe the records would be sealed, not open to the public. But Emma wasn't the public. If there had been a baby, it was probably her!

She put the sheet back into the opened envelope and pushed both pieces of mail into her pocket. She was going to be late. As soon as class ended, she was heading back to Juniper Street; no beach time for her today. But she'd better run back to her room first and collect her forgotten backpack with her textbook before she hurried to the class building.

Emma retraced her steps, still deep in thought. When she reached her floor, she looked down the straight corridor and paused.

A tall man in a dark suit stood in front of her room; the door was open, and she heard the murmur of voices. Was this Sophie's dad? He didn't look much like her roommate.

Emma walked closer, and a few feet from the door, the words became clearer; she heard her name spoken. He was asking about Emma Carter!

She made a small instinctive sound, a whimper of alarm, deep in her throat. The man must have heard. He turned to gaze directly at her. Above his immaculate white shirt and dark tie, his expression was set, plastic in its hardness, and his eyes were cold and impersonal. But when he saw her, emotion cracked the mask of his face, and Emma saw something—recognition? Triumph?

Emma felt a wave of fear wash over her, stark unthinking panic that took her by surprise, sent her whirling and running back up the hall toward the outer door. She knew she had to get away, she had to escape—though she didn't know why.

She ran.

Chapter
Fifteen

"Wait!"

She heard the man shout, but Emma didn't hesitate. She had never been so terrified. She pushed through the outer door and ran. But he was so close—so close—

Then she saw the concrete stairwell that she and Sophie had used one night—the service tunnel! Without pausing to think, Emma hurtled down the stairwell, slipped through the metal door and shut it softly behind her. Then she ran through the poorly lit corridor, feeling a blast of hot air from pipes that hung near the ceiling, hoping not to meet some half-crazed street person lingering here. Though no one would have frightened her more than the man in the dorm.

She heard no sound of pursuit. Had she lost him? Slowing her frantic run, Emma saw an exit she recognized. She climbed another set of steps and came back out into the sunshine, near the edge of the campus. Breathing hard, she looked around, then stopped in the shade of an oak tree, her legs folding as she collapsed onto the grass. Her heart pounded so hard it shook her whole body, and she gasped for air, chest heaving.

Who was that man? Why was he seeking her?

She didn't want to know the answer. And now she was afraid to go to class. Would Sophie have told him what class they had together? He might come to the classroom. Emma felt panic threaten again.

She stood up, her legs still wobbly, and walked away from the campus to the coffee shop where she and Luke often stopped for muffins before going to the beach. She had no money left to buy anything; she still hadn't picked up her backpack. Now what? She sat down at one of the booths, not sure what to do next.

When a waitress came up, Emma said, "I'm waiting for someone."

The woman nodded and left; the ploy would buy a little time. Emma had to decide what to do. She couldn't take the bus crosstown until she had retrieved her backpack with her wallet and money, but she was afraid to go back to her room. What if the stranger was still there, waiting for her?

She pressed her trembling hands together and tried to push back her fear. What was going on? Who was the man in the dark suit?

She sat there for a long time, feeling the waitress's curious gaze occasionally, but the shop was mostly empty, and no one asked her to leave.

Emma was staring down at her clasped hands when she felt a rush of air as the door opened and shut. She looked up quickly at the sight of a tall male form outlined by bright sunlight. She jerked to her feet, ready to run, but he came closer, and she saw jeans and a T-shirt instead of a dark suit. Then he walked out of the glare and she could make out his face.

"Luke!" she said, weak with relief. She sat down again, feeling limp with her unexpected reprieve.

"Emma, you okay?" He slipped into the other side of the booth. "Sophie said—"

Emma shuddered. "What? He was asking about me. Who was he?"

Luke's expression was serious. "He said he was FBI, Emma. What's going on?"

She gasped. "Are you sure?"

"Sophie said he showed her an ID. Why would the FBI be asking to speak to you?"

"I think it's about Leigh," Emma said slowly. She told Luke again about the poster in the post office. "She was wanted for murder; I guess she still is."

Luke nodded. "It's not like stealing a car," he pointed out. "A murder charge is forever, I guess. How did he know you were looking for Leigh, too?"

Emma shook her head. "I don't know. But Karyl, the woman at the dry cleaners, she said they had questioned her—do you think her phone is tapped?"

Luke shrugged. Emma felt a moment of disbelief; this was something that happened to people in TV shows, not in real life. She looked down at the much-scrubbed wood table beneath her hands, trying to ground herself in reality. She looked at her wristwatch, then realized something.

"Class isn't even over. You didn't go?"

Luke's eyes were dark with concern. "Sophie came in all upset, and when she told me—I thought I'd better try to find you. I checked all the spots on campus I could think of, then I thought of this place."

Emma remembered the envelopes in her jeans' pocket. "I got the birth certificate! I was going back to Juniper Street to check the new address, but my backpack is still in the dorm. I'm afraid to go back, but I don't have money for the bus fare."

Luke stood up. "I have enough; let's go."

"But—maybe you shouldn't get involved," Emma said, not wanting to give up the security of his presence, but worried about Luke getting into trouble, too. But she hadn't done anything!

"What are friends for?" he said, his tone half-joking. "Not just for the good times, right?"

She smiled at him, wanting to throw her arms around him and hug him tightly, but there were more customers now in the coffee shop, and anyhow, there was no time to waste. Emma had to find the answers she sought, before the authorities found her.

What would they do? Probably ask questions, Emma thought as she and Luke walked up to the bus stop. She didn't really want to explain how she had gotten interested in the mystery woman, the protestor/terrorist/murder suspect. Was Emma really the daughter of a murderer? The thought left her cold inside. No, she wasn't sure yet, but she couldn't stop, now. Emma had to know the truth.

They caught the next bus, and when they reached Juniper, walked to the street number on the birth certificate. She had canvassed the 500 block the first time she came to Juniper Street, but not this block.

But she was disappointed again. Emma looked over the small shopping complex that took up the 480s site. If there had once been apartment buildings at 489, they had been demolished long ago. Swallowing her disappointment, she pushed open the glass door and went into a small boutique.

"Can I help you?" a saleslady asked.

"Do you know how long the store has been here?" Emma asked. "And what was on the site before this block of shops was built?"

The clerk, who wasn't that much older than Emma, looked confused. "Uh, no," she said. She glanced back at the counter. "You might ask Mrs. Lee."

But the other salesperson knew a little more. "I've been here ten years," the woman said. "It was here some time before that. Why do you want to know?"

"I'm trying to find a Leigh Grimble," Emma explained. "I think she lived her twenty years ago."

The woman shrugged, losing interest. "That's a long time," she pointed out unnecessarily. "I'm afraid we can't help you."

Sighing, Emma tried the next store, with Luke a comforting presence by her side. They spent the rest of the morning in a slow, tedious survey of the surrounding stores, but no one remembered any apartments.

"Come on, let's get something to eat," Luke said finally. "It's almost two. And I bet you had nothing for breakfast; you look about to fall over."

Emma wanted to argue, but she did feel hollow inside. It wasn't just hunger; she was losing her very essence. She might not be the person she had always thought she was. Where did that leave her? And if they found no trace of Leigh Grimble, would she ever know?

Luke led the way up a side street to a small deli; they ordered sandwiches and colas, and Luke paid for the food. Then they sat down at a tiny table. Emma gazed at her sandwich, almost too weary to take the first bite.

"Eat, you'll feel better," Luke urged, taking a big bite of his own lunch.

She picked up the roll and nibbled, chewing slowly. They ate for a few minutes in silence.

"If I could just find someone who remembered the apartments at 489—" Emma began, when a thin voice from behind her broke in.

"You're looking for the Rosemead Building? It was taken down years ago, dearie. Didn't you know?"

Emma turned quickly. A tiny white-haired woman dressed in an improbable hot-pink tunic and stretch pants sat at the next table, daintily eating a salad.

"Do you remember the apartments?" Emma asked, hope surging back.

"Of course, I lived there for years till they tore the place down. But it was crumbling already, so it really wasn't a loss." The old woman took another birdlike bite. "I found a much nicer apartment, even if they do keep raising the rent, drat them."

"Did you know a girl named Leigh Grimble, or any of her family?"

"Oh, her family wasn't anyone you'd want to know. Nasty man, her father, and that's all she had."

The woman's eyes, bright with intelligence, focused on Emma. "My, you look a lot like her, dearie, did you know that? Is she a relative?"

"I'm trying to find out," Emma admitted, feeling her pulse pound. "You do remember her, then?"

"Oh, yes, a sweet thing, Leigh, when she wasn't marching in those silly protests. She used to walk my little dog for me when my knee acted up."

Emma was unexpectedly moved; Leigh might be her mother. It was comforting to hear that someone had thought well of her, that Leigh herself had been capable of kindness, not just the rage so often captured in the newspaper photos. But the next question was crucial.

"Have you seen her lately?" Emma could barely get the words out; her throat was suddenly tight.

The woman shook her head. "Oh no, not after the explosion. You know about that?"

Emma nodded, disappointment rushing back like an ocean wave, drowning her spark of hope.

The elderly woman's gaze was sympathetic. "It was all because of the man, you know. I don't believe Leigh would have hurt anyone—if she did—on her own."

"What man?" Emma's voice sounded rusty.

"Oh, that Tony person." The woman picked up her fork again. "He wasn't very nice. You'd think poor Leigh would have noticed that, after living with her father, but then—they say girls tend to do that, pick up a bad sort, I mean, when that's all they know."

Emma swallowed hard again, almost sick that this un-expected lead had led her no closer to finding Leigh. Was it true that Leigh was dead? If so, Emma's search was hopeless. Maybe she should just accept that.

Emma had lost her appetite; she waited for Luke to fin-ish his lunch, then she thanked the woman at the next table and stood up. Suddenly, she wanted to get away from this street with its troubling echoes.

Luke didn't question her until they had walked two blocks back toward a bus stop. "Now what?"

"I think—I think I should go back to the library and look for a death certificate," Emma said, her shoulders heavy. She had come all this way, and she still was no closer to finding Leigh Grimble, or the truth about Emma's birth.

Luke put one arm lightly around her shoulders, and she leaned against him as they waited for the bus. No, the trip had gained her something—she had met Luke. She wasn't sure she could have endured this painful combing through the past without his friendship.

On the way back to Westwood, she remembered the man from the FBI, and her nervousness returned.

"Let's try the public library first," she told Luke, not wanting to go back to the campus. The Feds had somehow tracked her to the dorm; she wanted to avoid going back to her room as long as she could.

They got off the bus at an earlier stop and found the nearest branch library. When they walked in the door, Emma glanced at a rack of magazines and stopped so abruptly that Luke walked into her.

"Sorry," he said. "What?"

"I just remembered. Karyl said the group was in one of the news magazines; I've only looked at the newspa-per clippings," Emma said. "Let's see if we can find the article."

With the reference librarian's help, they tracked down

the issue of *Newsweek* that Emma sought, and she and Luke were soon bent over a microfilm machine. When the right page came up on the screen, Emma glanced at the headline: "Green Power Group in Trouble Again." Then, beside her, she felt Luke stiffen. "What is it?"

He stared at the photo that accompanied the article. It was in color, the first color picture she had seen of the environmental group. Leigh was there, holding a protest sign, with her long pale hair and dusty blue eyes, and Karyl, her hair untouched by gray, her features young, her eyes less bitter. Several other protestors clustered around them.

And Tony, the man who had led the group, stood just behind the women, his lips twisted into a grimace. But it was his eyes that held Emma, his eyes that had made Luke freeze in surprise.

The man had striking blue-green eyes, aqua eyes that jumped off the page.

Eyes the color of Emma's.

Chapter
Sixteen

Emma jumped up, hearing a strangled sound that she didn't recognize at first had come from her own lips.

"Emma, wait," she heard Luke call, but she was running, running away from her moment of truth: truth she had sought so hard to find, and now truth that she didn't think she could bear.

She was outside the library before she paused, gasping, leaning against the low brick wall that surrounded the front of the building. Her knees felt weak; she sat down abruptly.

Luke found her there; he pulled her into his arms. The tears came so hard and fast that Emma had to struggle to get any words out.

"It's true, I really am adopted, and they never told me. I've lost my mother, and my father, as well. I'd thought about my mom not being my mom, but somehow, I never thought about that part of it—about my dad—stupid, huh?"

Luke patted her back. "Emma—"

"It's just, I have the greatest dad," Emma said, her voice thick with tears. "And now I've lost him, too." She sobbed, unable to say anything more; Luke hugged her tightly.

"Emma, you haven't lost them. I don't know why they didn't tell you, but your dad is still your dad, your mom is still your mom."

Emma shook her head. "But everything is different; my real father was a murderer, Luke! And my real mother helped him. What does that make me? I don't know who I am, anymore. Am I a terrible person, too? I feel so lost." She shut her eyes, rubbing them, uselessly trying to stop the tears.

Luke still held her; without the support of his arms wrapped around her, she felt as if she might fly apart into wild and random atoms, as disconnected as the stranger she had suddenly become. He was all that kept her whole, and he spoke soothing words into her ear, soft words whose meaning she didn't even notice. It was the feel of his arms around her, the soft tone of his voice that mattered.

At last the tears slowed, and she scrubbed at her face, wishing for a tissue, embarrassed that her nose was running and she had nothing to wipe it with.

She dug into her pocket but had to resort to the envelope that Leigh's birth certificate had come in. The stiff paper didn't make a very good handkerchief, but it was better than nothing.

"Don't you think it's time you talked to your parents?" Luke asked, his voice quiet.

Emma nodded, feeling incredibly weary. "Yes, I have to go home."

His brows lifted in surprise. "But our class—"

"I know." She didn't mind leaving the class, but the thought of flying away from Luke made her wince. "I can't sort this out over the phone, Luke. I have to look them in the eye—find out what they were thinking, not to tell me all this. I just can't wait. I'm sorry, I hate to leave so soon, but—"

He nodded, but his lips turned down. "I'm going to miss you, Emma. I can't believe how much."

She leaned into his arms, thankful for the solid strength of him, the kindness in his eyes. "Me, too," she whispered.

They walked the rest of the way back to the campus, and—feeling absurd, but still nervous, Emma loitered a half block away from the dorm while Luke walked up to the door, opened it and peered into the hall. He nodded to Emma, and she hurried across the grass.

"No sign of him," Luke reported. "I'll wait for you here."

He'd already announced he was going to the airport with her, and she didn't try to argue. The thought of not seeing Luke again was another pain amid a whole chorus of misery that played in the back of her mind.

The dorm room was empty, and their class would have ended by now. Had Sophie gone to the beach again or was she out somewhere eating lunch? Emma was sorry she couldn't say good-bye. She pulled her clothes out of the bureau drawers and the closet, cramming them all hastily into her suitcase, grabbing shampoo and makeup. She zipped her suitcase shut, pulled her backpack onto her arm, and scribbled a quick note to her roommate, which she left on the desk for Sophie to find later.

Emma also wrote a few lines on another slip of paper, then pushed it into her pocket just as the phone rang. She jumped, but couldn't bring herself to answer.

Instead, peering cautiously into the hall, with her suitcase pulling on one arm, and the backpack with her wallet and return ticket in the other, Emma ran for the outer door. Maybe the FBI agent would never look for her again, maybe all this haste was for nothing. But she couldn't forget the look in the man's eyes when he had first seen her— she wasn't taking any chances.

Outside the dorm, Luke lifted her suitcase and they walked quickly to the bus stop. Emma was thankful to have Luke with her. When they reached Los Angeles International Airport, Emma went to the ticket counter and stood in line to change her ticket. The ticket agent put her on standby, checked in her suitcase, and gave her the correct gate number.

Emma walked with Luke up to the security gate, then stopped, reluctant to say good-bye.

"I'm sorry about what you learned," Luke told her. "I hate that you'll go home with bad memories of Los Angeles. I was hoping you might come back. UCLA is a great college, you know."

"All my memories aren't bad," she offered, suddenly feeling shy. "I'm so glad I met you—that was the best part of my trip."

"Good," he said simply and leaned to kiss her.

The touch of his lips made her heart seem to contract. Would she ever see him again? Emma felt a lump in her throat unconnected to the turmoil that filled the rest of her life. When they pulled apart, she reached into her pocket. "This is my home address and phone number," she told him. "I hope you don't forget me."

"Never," he promised. "Will you let me know what happens, about your parents, I mean? I don't want to think about you being unhappy. It'll work out, Emma."

She sighed. "I hope so." She glanced at the row of monitors on the wall behind him. "I'd better go and see if I can get on this flight." She clung to him for one more minute, then released him, trying to smile.

Luke stepped back, his own smile twisted.

Emma wanted to say more, but wasn't sure what the words should be. She turned and dumped her backpack on the rolling belt for the X-ray machine to scan, then walked through the security gate. The backpack was innocent, but if they could look inside of her, she thought bitterly, what would they see? Daughter of a murderer—two murderers? This was the legacy she was left with.

Emma found the right gate and waited impatiently for the ticketed passengers to board the plane, then at last they called her name and she was able to walk on board, finding a seat toward the back of the aircraft.

The flight seemed very long; Emma was too agitated to sleep or to eat the pitiful excuse of a dinner the flight attendants served.

Once, tears threatened to overwhelm her again. Emma dug into her pocket for a tissue, but she found only the copy of Leigh Grimble's birth certificate, and something else.

It was the second envelope, the one with her mom's birth certificate. She'd had no time to look up her mother's birthplace, after all, and Emma almost pushed the envelope back into her pocket still unopened. But curiosity stirred—her mom had never said much about her first home—and Emma ripped the edge and pulled out the paper inside.

But it was not a copy of a birth certificate, as she had expected. Instead, it was almost blank, and at the top, the form read: "No birth record on file for this name."

Emma blinked; had she filled out the form wrong? What did it mean? She stared at the sheet of paper, but her brain couldn't cope with more mysteries. Nothing made sense anymore.

On the panel above her head, the seat belt sign blinked on, and the intercom blared, "Please be sure your seats are in an upright position and all tray tables are stowed as we prepare for landing. Please fasten your seat belts . . ."

Emma clicked her seat belt shut and lay back against the seat. Soon, she would be home; her parents—*her parents*—didn't even know she was coming home early. What would she say to them?

The plane dipped, and her stomach rolled with the motion. She stared out the window at a sky turning lavender with the approaching sunset. Beneath the plane, green fields gave way to paved streets and clumps of tiny buildings, growing larger and closer together as they neared Chicago. The buildings grew in size as the plane circled into position for landing.

Soon, she would know the rest of the story.

When at last the plane taxied into its allotted slot, Emma grabbed her backpack and stood, eager to get out of this claustrophobic aisle and on her way. After long minutes, the line ahead of her moved, and she made her way off the plane and found the luggage turnstiles where she waited for her suitcase. Around her, passengers greeted friends and hugged relatives; it made the loneliness inside her even harder to bear.

She had enough cash to take a shuttle van out to Oak Grove. Emma was both eager and frightened to see her home for the first time in weeks. It felt as if she'd been away for years; she could hardly remember the person she used to be, concerned only with dates and new clothes and maybe college applications. That girl had had a loving, stable family, and she'd not even appreciated them.

When the van pulled up in front of her comfortable brick home, Emma gazed at it as if she had never seen it before. She was coming home a different person from the girl who had left for California; she had birth parents she had never known, a history she had never suspected; she had a façade of lies where she had expected only solid foundations of love and trust.

The van driver retrieved her suitcase from the back of the van before he returned to his seat and pulled the vehicle away. Emma pulled her bag up the driveway, leaving it on the front porch. She used her key to open the front door, then stepped inside.

She could hear voices from the kitchen. Were they all having dinner, her dad, her mom, her brothers? She heard a patter of nails on the hardwood floor, and then Happy dashed up the hall, his tail wagging.

She patted him briefly but couldn't linger. Dropping her backpack in the hall, Emma walked slowly toward the kitchen, dreading now her first sight of her family—or the people she had thought were her family.

They were all seated in the breakfast nook; Ethan saw her first. "Emma!" he exclaimed in surprise.

All the other heads turned, and her mom gasped.

Her dad blinked. "Emma, what are you doing home? Did something happen to your class?"

All the way home, all through that interminable flight, cramped in her narrow seat, Emma had rehearsed what she would say, trying a dozen different phrases. And now she could remember none of them. Her throat ached again; the lump was back. She wanted to shout at her parents, but when the words came out, they were almost a whisper.

"Why didn't you tell me?" she said.

Her dad frowned in bewilderment. Emma turned to her mom, who looked pale, her eyes stricken. "Why didn't you tell me I was adopted?"

One of her brothers made a funny noise, but she didn't look at the boys; she was still watching her mother. "You could have told me."

"Emma, you're not adopted," her dad was saying. "What's going on?"

But her mother hadn't answered; her cheeks were so white that her pale blue eyes seemed to darken by contrast.

"Why didn't you tell me you weren't my mom, that Dad—Dad isn't my dad?" Emma said. "I saw the pictures. Why didn't you tell me about the murder charge?"

Her mother made a small strangled sound, deep in her throat, and Emma heard her father gasp.

"Elizabeth?" he breathed.

Emma heard the surprise, the pain in the single word, and she jerked her head back to stare at him in shock.

He didn't know, oh God, her father hadn't known, either? How was it possible? He gazed at her mother as if he'd never seen her before, and he half-rose, then fell back into his chair. His face had flushed, and he put one hand to his chest.

"Dad!" one of the boys shouted.

"Oh, dear God," her mother exclaimed. "Emma, call 9-1-1, now, quick!"

What had she done? Emma ran to the phone on the kitchen wall as her mother hurried to stand over her dad, throwing her arms around him.

Emma found her hands shaking, she could hardly punch the right buttons. The phone rang and rang—why did it take so long—this was an emergency. Where were these people? Wasn't anyone there?

At last, the connection was made. Emma yelled into the phone. "We need an ambulance; my dad is having a heart attack! Hurry, hurry!"

The voice on the other end of the line was asking questions; Emma tried to answer, but she watched her father anxiously. He mumbled something as he bent over his plate, his face now almost gray.

"Oh, hurry, please," Emma said into the phone again. "My dad's dying!"

Her mother knelt beside her husband, both arms around him. Sobbing, Ethan crouched in his chair; he had turned over his glass of milk. The liquid dripped steadily to the tile floor, and no one else even noticed. Todd's face was tight with alarm and fear. Happy whined, pawing at Emma's leg.

Oh, God, had she killed him? Please, please don't die, she thought, grasping the phone like a lifeline. "Hurry!" she repeated.

Where were the paramedics? They were supposed to

come quickly; it seemed forever since she'd made the call. Her father's breath came in labored gasps; she could hear it in the awful stillness. Ethan wept almost silently, and her mother murmured words to her husband that Emma couldn't hear.

At last, someone pounded on the front door. Thank heavens! Emma dropped the phone and ran for the front door and the life-saving aid beyond it.

She grabbed the handle and pulled open the door. Instead of the uniformed paramedic she had expected, she saw a tall figure in a dark suit.

Emma stepped back, shock hitting her like a fist into her stomach. It was the man from the dorm. But he had been in California—how—

"Is this the residence of Elizabeth Carter?" the man demanded. His eyes were so cold.

"I—wait, no—" Emma tried to say, but he had already pushed past her, and there were more men behind him, another man in a suit, and policemen in blue uniforms.

They strode into the house, and Emma could only run after them, uttering words of protest that no one heeded. The men marched into the kitchen, hardly pausing at the sight of her father slumped over the table, her mother's arms still circling him.

"Leigh Grimble, also known as Elizabeth Carter," the agent said, "you're under arrest."

Chapter
Seventeen

Emma felt her legs turn rubbery; she couldn't even make it to a chair. She leaned against the kitchen cabinet and slipped slowly to the cold tile floor. While the FBI agent put handcuffs—*handcuffs!*—on her mother, while her brothers cried out loud as if they were babies, while a policeman finally bent over her dad—she curled up into a ball, shut her eyes, and put her hands over her ears, as if she could stop this terrible scene by not listening, by not seeing.

Time stretched. When she opened her eyes again, the paramedics were there at last; they were putting her dad onto a stretcher, and a policeman bent over Ethan, saying something into his ear. Todd was clinging to their dad's hand, and one of the uniformed men gently pulled him away.

Her mother was gone, and so were the federal agents. Where was her mother?

The men behind the stretcher wheeled her father out.

She couldn't see his face. He had a mask over his mouth; was he breathing?

She shut her eyes again, put her hands over her ears.

Time passed. People were speaking; she didn't hear the words. Someone shook her arm.

She opened her eyes reluctantly. A policeman bent over her; he had dark skin, and his brows were knit low over deep brown eyes. "Miss, we need to call someone to stay with you and your brothers. Is there a relative we can call?"

She stared at him blankly; she heard his words, but they made no sense. Her brain was frozen.

"A relative in town, or a neighbor? Who do you want to come and stay with you?"

"Uncle Don," she heard Todd say clearly. "I want Uncle Don."

Her father's brother, some distant part of her mind tried to explain. But her lips didn't move. The officer turned with relief to Todd, who dialed the number.

In a moment, Emma heard her brother speaking on the phone, his voice hoarse with the tears he'd shed. How long had it been since she'd seen Todd cry? His face was still streaked with tear tracks.

Emma couldn't cry; she felt numb. She had thought she'd lost her mother and her father, had come home vibrant with anger and hurt. And now she had lost them all over again, and destroyed her little brothers' happiness, as well.

She was a terrible person. Emma shut her eyes and leaned her head against her knees. The pain hovered just outside of her vision, too close, too close. It was so great, she was afraid to let it in.

Later, she heard a familiar voice, and for a moment, she thought her dad had returned. She opened her eyes, blinking, hoping it had all been a terrible nightmare—maybe she was still on the plane, still circling Chicago. Maybe she could take it all back, make the police go away, keep the terrible secrets from her mother's past closed up and hidden.

But it was her uncle, not her father; their voices sounded a little bit the same. He was on his knees beside her; his expression was grave. How could he bear to look at her? She had made her father ill, sent her mother to prison. Except Russell Carter wasn't really her father—oh, God, how could she live with that? Anger stirred again, beneath the numbness of her shock.

"Emma?" her uncle said. "Can you hear me? I think you should go lie down; I've called a doctor."

She didn't want a doctor. Looking past him for a moment, Emma saw her aunt Claire at the kitchen table, her arms about the two boys. Ethan's eyes were red with weeping; Todd looked sullen.

He caught Emma's gaze, and Todd's face flushed. "It's your fault, Emma!" he shouted at her from across the kitchen. "I hate you! It's all your fault!"

Emma swallowed hard and couldn't answer. Her aunt shushed her brother, and her uncle pulled her gently to her feet. "Come on, Emma; let's take you to your room. I want you to lie down until the doctor calls back."

She allowed him to lead her to the stairs and up to her own room, which had a strange, empty feel to it. She lay across the top of the spread, and her uncle went into the bathroom to get her a glass of water.

Later, they brought a pill to swallow, and she didn't try to resist. It didn't matter; nothing mattered anymore. Her eyes drifted shut.

When she opened her eyes again, she found herself beneath the sheets, and she knew she had slept. Someone had pulled off her shoes and jeans; she still wore the crumbled T-shirt from yesterday, and the same underwear and socks.

For a moment, she blinked against the daylight, then all the memories flooded back. Emma groaned.

Oh, God, what had she done?

Her father! Or the man she'd always thought was her father—what did she call him now? Russell Carter, Dr. Russell Carter, who had saved so many lives—whose two sons needed him. Was he still alive? Had he died while Emma slept? She would be a murderer, too. No one would believe that she cared, how much she cared, not when she had made him sick.

Oh, please, God, she prayed silently, afraid to call out, afraid to hear one more shattering answer. Please, let him be alive. Let him be all right.

She pushed herself up, feeling groggy and weak, made it to the bathroom, then washed her face and hands. She found a robe on the back of the bathroom door and tied it around her.

The house seemed very quiet. Emma made her way downstairs, clinging to the banister—she still felt weak and disoriented—wondering if everyone else was gone. Maybe they had all left her, she thought with a return of the self-hatred that had made her ill with guilt last night. Who would want her for family, after this?

At last, she heard the scrabble of flying feet and Happy rushed up to her, his tail wagging as if he, too, feared being alone. She stopped to hug the dog. "Oh, Happy, at least you still love me."

Her aunt looked out of the kitchen. "You're awake. But you're awfully pale. Come and sit down, Emma, how do you feel?"

Emma didn't want to meet her aunt's eye. How could she be nice; didn't she know what Emma had done?

"My—my dad?" Emma whispered, "what—"

"He's doing much better," her aunt said quickly. "It was only a mild attack; he'll probably stay in the hospital another few days, though, to be safe. Your uncle took the boys up to see him; they were so worried."

Emma couldn't hold back the tears of relief. She put her

hands up to hide her face, and she cried and cried. Her aunt patted her shoulder until the sobbing slowed, then went to the refrigerator. "You need to eat something, Emma. How about some scrambled eggs?"

Emma nodded. She was too empty inside to care about food, but she knew her aunt was trying to be helpful.

"And my mom?" she whispered at last.

Her aunt's expression wavered for an instant, then she looked determinedly cheerful again. "Don called one of the partners in his firm. She has a good lawyer, Emma. So far, the court has refused to release her on bond, but we'll do everything we can."

Why? Emma wondered as her aunt pulled eggs and butter out of the fridge and turned toward the stove. Why were her dad's relatives helping her mom? Didn't they know all this misery had occurred because of her?

The parts to the puzzle that had taken so long to fall into place now seemed obvious. Emma felt anger burn inside her, thinking of seventeen years of lies. It was almost enough to fill the emptiness, almost.

When her aunt put a plate in front of her, Emma ate a few bites of the egg and toast, then pushed it back.

"Can I go see my—my dad?" she asked.

"Of course, dear. Why don't you take a shower, first? It might make you feel better," her aunt suggested.

Which was better than pointing out how grungy she looked, Emma thought. "Sure."

She went into the hall, and the dog followed, then ran away from her toward the front door.

"You need to go out? Just a minute." Emma went slowly to the door and put her hand on the latch. She had pushed it open before she heard her aunt call, "No, Emma! Don't open the door!"

Why not?

The wave of light and noise hit her like an avalanche, strobes flashing, TV and still cameras pointing at her, all focused on Emma in her second-best housecoat, with her hair matted and her eyes still swollen from weeping. Happy whined and snarled and ran between her legs back into the house.

"Did you know your mother was wanted for murder?" someone shouted into her face. "Did your father know? Did he help her?"

"How do you feel right now?" another voice yelled.

"Did you turn her in to the FBI?" a third person called.

They were running forward, well-dressed men and women with cruel, eager faces, microphones thrust out before them. Emma couldn't move; she felt herself shudder with fear as they came like a wave, ready to engulf her.

Chapter
Eighteen

Emma jumped back and slammed the door. She thought she heard a clunk as if the door had struck someone's mike, or a too-close camera. She hoped it hurt. Gasping, she leaned back against the doorframe. Her aunt hurried down the hallway.

"Oh dear, I should have warned you. There's newspeople and cameras all around the house, Emma. Don't open any of the doors, and don't answer the phone."

Emma saw that the phone in the hallway was off the hook; she hadn't identified the annoying buzz before.

Shuddering, Emma heard the clamor outside die down again, but the reporters were waiting; she knew they were waiting, like vultures, just as patient and unfeeling.

Her aunt took her arm. "Go shower and dress, dear, and we'll go to the hospital."

Nodding, Emma headed for the stairs. When she was ready, her mom's car was in the garage. Her aunt took the keys from the hall table without comment, and they got inside before her aunt opened the garage door. Then, as soon as it lifted, she backed rapidly out into the drive, turning with difficulty as the reporters with their cameras surged up, blocking their way.

Emma shrank back into her seat, wishing she could hide beneath it. Her aunt's lips were pressed into a tight line.

"Get away!" she called, but the cameras pushed forward, lights flashing, and she had to back almost into them before she could turn the car and pull out through the swelling mass of news media into the street.

Emma glanced back, thinking about her neighbors up and down the street. These people had known her family since she was in kindergarten; what were they thinking, now? Her mother's arrest would be on the news, all her friends at school would know about it.

How could she ever face her friends again? Emma groaned beneath her breath.

"I'm sure Russell will be all right," her aunt said, glancing her way.

Emma was ashamed of herself for thinking about anything besides her dad's condition. If she had no friends left, what else did she deserve?

More reporters lurked at the hospital, but this time a policeman managed to keep them back while Emma darted into the doorway. Her aunt drove on to the hospital parking garage to leave the car. "Go up to the third floor," her aunt told Emma before she got out of the car. "Look for the Cardiac Unit."

Emma knew where to go. She hurried to the elevator and pressed the button. She had been to the hospital with her dad many times, to help out at the children's Christmas party when her mom always made cookies and—no, she didn't want to think about that. But on other visits, her father had always been beside her, strong and confident in his white coat, not in danger himself.

When the elevator doors rolled back, she braced herself,

fearing more press, but she saw only a hospital security guard. A nurse at the station recognized her.

"Oh, Emma, your dad's coming along nicely, dear. And those terrible reporters! We're not allowing them up here, but you might wait in the staff lounge, just in case. As soon as your uncle and brothers come out of your dad's room, you can go in. We can't let too many people in at once."

Emma nodded; she really wanted to see her dad—Russell—alone. "Thank you," she said. She pushed open the door marked STAFF ONLY and went inside.

She had been in the staff lounge, too; when she was small, the nurses used to save her cookies and pieces of cake. The thought made her swallow hard. If she wasn't Russell Carter's daughter, who on earth was she?

The small room was empty right now; all the nurses were at their stations. A coffeemaker sat on a side table, with an empty box of doughnuts. The air smelled like coffee and antiseptic. A TV hummed at the side of the room; the volume was turned down, but when she heard a familiar voice, Emma turned quickly to look.

A reporter held out a microphone, and it was Jay's handsome face the camera focused upon.

"Oh, I hardly knew her," Jay was saying. "I mean, we were friends, classmates really. We dated a few times, nothing serious; it didn't mean a thing."

Emma felt the hurt rise inside her; Jay's expression was so unconcerned, his voice so uncaring. Nothing serious, he said. This was the same guy who had wanted to take her to a motel room after the senior dance, she thought grimly.

Because of her dad, she hadn't gone; she couldn't go home and face her father, after all his lectures about waiting for sex, waiting until she was older, knew more about what she wanted.

She was glad now she hadn't had sex with Jay, who stood in front of the cameras and cast her aside so blithely.

"It didn't mean a thing," she muttered to the screen. "Yes, you're so right."

She walked across the room as the news channel switched to the courthouse. She saw her mother, her face pale, her eyes strangely blank, standing before a judge. "Held on a charge of conspiracy and accessory to murder," the reporter was saying. *Murder.*

Her gentle, quiet, charity-worker mother. It had all been a pose, then, a lie. Emma swallowed; she felt so much anger, so much betrayal that she could hardly hold it back. Her mother had lied to them all; Emma thought she might never be able to look at her again.

If they sent Elizabeth—Leigh—to prison, Emma wouldn't have to. How many years did a person get for murder? Karyl had served only four years, and she was still bitter.

Emma hit the switch hard, and the screen went black, then she walked up and down, too restless to sit. At last, the head nurse looked into the room. "You can go in now, Emma."

Her uncle and her two brothers were in the hall. Ethan ran up to hug her, and she held him tightly, but Todd frowned at her and stepped back instead. "You shouldn't be here," he muttered. "You want to give him another heart attack?"

"Todd." Uncle Don cleared his throat. "You know what your father said."

What had he said? Did he blame her, too? Suddenly, Emma was afraid to go into the room. But the nurse was holding the door, and Ethan released her.

"We'll wait for you in the staff lounge, Emma," her uncle said.

She had to go in. Emma drew a deep breath and walked into the tiny hospital room.

Clicking, blinking machines stood all around the bed, and she saw that her father had a tube of oxygen inserted into his nose. That must hurt, she thought, cringing. His eyes were shut, and his skin was so pale that she felt frightened all over again. They all said he was getting better, but what if they were wrong? Doctors were sometimes wrong, she knew that. She'd seen her father—seen Russell himself agonize over losing a patient.

She took another step closer to the bed, wanting to touch his hand, which lay outside the sheet, an IV needle going into his skin beneath the tape that held it in place. But she was afraid. She didn't know what to say, or what to do. Maybe he was asleep, tired after the boys' visit, and she should just go away and let him rest.

His eyelids fluttered, then opened. He blinked and lifted his hand slightly. "Emma," he muttered.

She wanted to touch his fingers, but she was afraid she would jerk the IV and hurt him. She gave a little wave instead.

"Are you okay?" she whispered.

"Not so bad," he said. His voice sounded strange; did the tube go all the way down his throat? Emma shivered at the thought. "Not as bad as I look, I'm sure."

Emma felt her eyes fill, and her vision blurred. She blinked hard. "I'm sorry," she said, still whispering. "I thought you knew. I'm so sorry."

He sighed. "Me, too."

Silence stretched like a steel cord; it seemed impossible to break. He looked so tired. But she couldn't go away, not yet.

"I figured it out, you know," she said softly. "When I was fourteen, I looked at your marriage license, at the date, and at my birth certificate . . . I knew Mom was pregnant with me when you married. I thought it was sort of romantic."

"Not the best way to start out," her dad said gruffly, "but worth it, in the long run."

"But now—do you want me to leave?" she asked, her

voice very low. She didn't want anyone else to hear his answer.

"Not till the nurse runs you out," he said, trying to smile. "We have a few minutes yet."

"No, I mean, do you want me to leave home?"

He opened his eyes wider this time. "Emma, what are you talking about?"

"Because I'm not really your daughter," she said, choking a little on the words. "Because it was all a lie."

He reached for her, and this time she took his hand, felt the reassuring aliveness of his grip.

"Emma, don't talk nonsense. You are my daughter, wherever, whomever the sperm came from. Your mother told me that she wasn't sure, after she realized she was pregnant; I knew there had been someone else before we met. But when you were born, I loved you so much, I wanted it to be true that you were mine. So I never tried to find out; I didn't really think about it again."

She looked at him, at the tired hazel eyes, the slightly lined forehead, the mouth so accustomed to smiling. This was the man who had left work early to come to her soccer games or to film her dance recitals, to applaud the loudest and to always be there when she needed him. This was the man who had walked the floor with her when she was small and her stomach hurt, and her mother had had her arms full with a fretful baby brother. This was the man who had sent pink roses for her sixteenth birthday.

That other man—the one with the angry eyes and the long hair, the man who had murdered—his image had been burned into her brain, but now it faded just a little.

"You are my father," Emma whispered, clutching his hand more tightly. "You're the only father I ever want."

He gripped her fingers just as hard. "I love you, Emma. This is where you belong; don't even think about anything else. It wasn't all a lie. The love was true; that's what counts."

For a moment, she clung to his hand, her relief so strong that she had to fight back the tears.

After a time, she said, "Todd hates me, and I don't blame him."

Her dad tried to smile. "He'll get over it; give him time. It was a shock. I tried to talk to him. And we've got a good lawyer for your mother. They haven't set bail yet, but she's been a model citizen for almost twenty years. Surely that counts for something."

"You still want her to come home?" Emma asked slowly. "When she might be a murderer?"

Her dad looked away for an instant, then met her troubled gaze. "I didn't know about the murder charge, Emma. And they won't let her come to see me, so I haven't asked her—but I don't have to ask. I know Elizabeth—my wife—is not a killer."

"And you still love her?"

"After nearly twenty years, yes, Emma. I love her. Don't you?"

"I don't know," she told him, very low. "I don't know."

He sighed again and they sat silently until the nurse came to tell her their time was up.

Emma kissed her father's forehead.

"Come back tomorrow," he said.

She nodded. "I will."

When she went into the hall, Emma felt lighter, released from her worst fear. But another heaviness still weighed her down. And Todd glared at her when she met her uncle and aunt and brothers in the hallway, and he wouldn't talk to her on the ride home.

Emma rode silently, one arm around Ethan, who at least allowed her close to him, her face turned toward the inside of the car, averted from the prying eyes of the cameras when they turned into their drive.

The anger was still inside her, pushed into a tight ball for now, and despite the relief she felt that her father—*her father*—had not disowned her, Emma wasn't ready to deal with the feelings she had for her mother.

They drove into the garage and shut the door—the reporters didn't actually crowd into the garage, which was trespassing and illegal, but the lights popped and flashed until the door slammed shut.

"I think we should pack up some of your clothes and go to our house for a few days," their uncle said. "Maybe it would be a little less hectic, and we can lose at least some of the reporters."

"What about Happy?" Ethan asked in alarm.

"We'll take Happy, don't worry," Uncle Don said. "I'm sure he'd love to chase our cats."

Ethan grinned and went to collect the dog's bowl and food and leash.

Emma climbed the stairs and pulled open her closet, looking for some clean clothes to pack. Much of her stuff was still in her suitcase; she'd never had a chance to unpack it. As she folded clothes, she looked up and saw the prom picture on her bureau: she and Jay in their formal dress, smiling at the camera.

Just friends, he'd said. *It didn't mean a thing.* She turned the photo facedown and went back to her packing.

They waited until after dark to leave, as if they were all fugitives. When they pulled out of the garage, her uncle drove them around town for some time until he felt he had lost the reporters who had tried to follow their car.

"They'll probably find our address soon enough," Aunt Claire said softly. Her uncle shrugged.

At least for tonight, they had some peace, Emma thought as she helped her uncle unfold the sofa bed for the boys, while her aunt sent her brothers off to brush their teeth and wash their faces.

Emma lingered until they returned. She gave Ethan a good-night hug, but Todd turned away from her.

"I didn't mean for this to happen," she told her brother.

"I didn't mean for you—for everyone to get hurt. I didn't know how many people it was going to harm. Honest, Todd, I didn't."

He still wouldn't meet her eyes. Sighing, she said, "I love you, Todd, I love you, Ethan," and left the room.

Her aunt had given Emma her cousin John's room; he was away at college, and his posters stared down at her from the walls. When Emma crawled into bed, feeling strange to be in yet another unfamiliar bedroom, she picked up the phone on the bedside table and held it. She wanted to call Revi, but her best friend was still in Florida. Would Revi disown her, too?

Emma hesitated, then she leaned over and pulled her wallet out of her backpack, to find the number to Luke's dorm room. Had he seen the news about her mother's arrest? Would he still want to talk to her?

Her heart beating fast, Emma dialed.

Chapter
Nineteen

He answered almost at once.

"Luke?"

"Emma! I've been trying to call you, but your line is always busy. Are you okay?"

She bit her lip. "We've got the phone off the hook because of the press calling. You saw the news about my mother's arrest?"

"Yeah," he said. "That's tough. I'm sorry it worked out this way, Emma."

"I think I led them home to her," she said, feeling a surge of guilt she hadn't admitted to anyone else. "The FBI. I didn't do it on purpose."

"I know that."

"I didn't mean to get her locked up. I think about where she is now, one tiny room somewhere, like Karyl said. But yet at the same time I'm so angry at her for not telling us, for lying, for making up a whole new name, a new life."

"Maybe she wanted a new life, Em," he said slowly.

"Maybe." She drew a deep breath. "I wasn't sure if you'd still talk to me—a murderer's daughter."

"Idiot," he said cheerfully. He sounded so normal that she wanted to reach through the phone and hug him. "You're not responsible for what your mother did."

Or my father, she thought. No, *Tony*. Her father was lying in a hospital bed right now because of the actions of that angry, twisted man who had given her life, but who would never be her father. She pulled her thoughts back to Luke's comforting voice.

"It's you I care about, you know."

"You don't mind about the news, about the things they'll say?"

"I know you better than some stupid reporter," he told her. "Don't let them get you down, Emma."

"It's pretty bad, all the cameras, the shouting. They crowd around you like—like—"

"Like sharks on a dying whale," he suggested, his tone grim. "Try to pretend you're some glamorous movie star being chased by the paparazzi. Do a Greta Garbo imitation—"

"Who?" Emma demanded, smiling in spite of herself. She could never keep up with his store of movie trivia.

"A famous old movie star who didn't like the press," he explained. "She used to say, 'I just want to be alone.' "

"She had the right idea," Emma said, sighing. "I'll try."

"I wish I could be there to help you."

Emma did, too.

They talked for a while about the class, about what Sophie had said when she'd learned her roommate had left abruptly, about the film they would see in class tomorrow. It was normal and reassuring, and it made Emma feel as if some of her life had not been twisted apart.

"Thanks for talking," she said before they said good night.

"Call me again," Luke said. "I'll call you, too, as soon as your line is free."

When she hung up, Emma was able to shut her eyes, thinking about Luke instead of about the flashing cameras, and drift into sleep.

For the next two days they visited the hospital, where her father continued to improve, and most of the time they managed to evade the press. Her uncle picked up their mail and on Thursday he talked to the lawyer who was handling her mother's case.

"Your mother wants to see you, Emma," he told her quietly after he hung up the phone.

Emma was making sandwiches for her brothers. "I don't want to see her."

"I can't force you," her uncle said, "but I hope you change your mind."

That night, Emma couldn't sleep at all. She tossed and turned, feeling the anger inside her like a volcano, looking for any chance to erupt. What could she say to her mother, without shouting, without showing how much she despised the years of lying, the chances she'd taken with her husband's, her family's lives?

Emma lay awake in her cousin's bed until the darkness outside the window faded into dawn. Only then did she remember Karyl's words. Her father had died while she was in prison, the former protestor had said. And she'd never had the chance to speak to him again.

What if her mother went to prison, for real? What if Emma never got to see her? Was that really what she wanted?

The next day, after they visited the hospital, Emma took her uncle aside.

"I want to talk to my mother," she said.

Her uncle nodded. They took the boys home, and her uncle made several phone calls, then they set out again in the afternoon.

Emma was silent as they drove to the large building where her mother was being kept. She saw razor wire on top of the building's roof, and bars on the windows. Emma shivered when she looked at them, thinking about how they would look from the inside, from a room whose lock was on the other side of the door.

There were security people inside, and forms to fill out, and long hallways that smelled of cleaning fluid and other more unpleasant odors. The strong aromas made Emma feel sick to her stomach; was this what her mother saw, smelled, all day long, every day? She thought of her mother's bedroom at home: the soft rose-colored draperies and the comfortable pillow-topped bed. What must her mother be feeling, now?

The room where Emma was taken was small, with block walls and one table and two chairs. Her mother sat on one side of the table, dressed in an orange uniform. Her already gray hair seemed to have whitened overnight, and her skin looked sallow without any makeup.

Emma felt shocked despite herself. She walked in, feeling awkward, and sat down to face her mother.

"I'm glad you came, Emma," her mother said, her voice quiet.

"I didn't want to," Emma said, trying to hold on to her anger. But she hadn't expected to see her mother look so beaten, so defeated. "You lied to all of us! How could you do that?"

"I'm sorry, Emma, very sorry. It was the wrong thing to do." Elizabeth/Leigh Carter shut her eyes for a moment, pressing her lips together, and the gesture was so much like Emma's own habit that Emma had to take a deep breath. Her mother's face had been changed so much that the strong resemblance between the two of them had been obscured, but the small gestures remained, revealing their close relationship despite her mother's altered appearance.

"Try to understand," her mother went on. "You'll be eighteen in a few months; I was nineteen when it happened, not much older than you. I didn't have anyone at home who cared about me. I wanted friends, I wanted somewhere to belong, and I found the group; plus, I really thought I was helping the world. I thought I was doing the right thing, or at least, sometimes the wrong things but for the right reasons. I thought that made it okay."

"Even murder?" Emma blurted.

"No, no. I promise you, I didn't know about the bomb, I didn't know that he—that Tony was going to rob a bank." Her mom sat up straighter, her voice earnest.

Emma bit her lip.

"After the explosion, I was hurt pretty bad, but I got away from the police. I was running down the street and I ran straight into your dad—he was a medical student then—he tried to take me to the emergency room, but I wouldn't go. I told him I had been in the protest, and they might arrest me. I never told him my real name. I was scared, Emma; I just wanted to get away."

"Didn't he see the pictures on TV?" Emma demanded. "They were looking for you; your photo was in the news, in the papers. How could he not recognize you as Leigh River Greenleaf?"

Her mother grimaced. "You don't know what I looked like that day, Emma. My face was in pieces, my nose was broken, and my cheekbones—I had serious burns. Your dad helped me, and he was so kind, so sweet. I fell in love with him right away, I think. Later, much later, I had surgery on my face to cover some of the worst scars." She touched the side of her face where the burn marks still showed; it was a habit so old that Emma hardly noticed—until now, when she knew where the burns came from.

"I made up a new name, and I just never went back to my old neighborhood, never looked up the protest group again. I had nothing to go back for, really. After your dad got out of medical school, he got a residency back east, and I was happy to move with him; we had you by that time, and your dad—your dad was so crazy about you. I knew it was wrong to lie, but I thought I'd been given a new life, and I couldn't resist the chance to take it. I never meant to hurt everyone; I never realized how many people my lies would affect."

Her voice faded.

Emma remembered her own comments to Todd; she hadn't meant to hurt her family, either. She wanted to believe her mother, she had always believed her, but then, she knew now that her mother had been lying to her for years, by omission, by all the truths she had left unsaid, as well as by the stories she'd made up.

"You were never going to tell me about Tony?" Emma demanded.

"Are you happier, now that you know?" her mother countered.

It was Emma's turn to look away. She stared down at the mottled plastic top of the table and sighed. "Do you hate me?" she asked very quietly. "Because I led the FBI to you? I didn't mean to."

"Of course not," her mother said quickly. "Emma, for years, every time I heard a siren, my stomach turned over. I thought, this time, it might be for me. This time, maybe they had found me. I knew the knock on the door would come, some day. I'm just sorry that I hurt all of you, and I hope"—her voice wavered—"I hope I have the chance to try to make it up to you."

Emma looked up again and saw the tears on her mom's cheeks. For a moment, she couldn't answer, then the words came of their own volition.

"I hope you do, too."

A woman warden opened the door behind her mother and looked into the room. "Time's up," she said.

Her mother stood up reluctantly. "I'm not allowed to hug you, Emma, but remember that I love you. Tell them all—your brothers, your father—that I love them, and I'm so sorry."

"I will." Emma promised, her own voice husky. "Dad told me he still loves you."

Her mother's smile was wintery. "I couldn't live without him," she said simply. "And, Em, if you want to know more about what it was really like when I was your age"—she took a deep breath—"look in the small drawer of my desk. The key is in my jewelry box."

Then the security officer took her away, and Emma was taken back through two locked gates to where her uncle waited.

"You okay, Emmie?" he asked.

She bit her lip. "I will be, if they don't send her to jail forever. Do you think they will?"

"I don't know," her uncle said. "I hope not."

They drove to her uncle and aunt's home in silence, but Emma remembered her mother's last enigmatic comment, and she asked to go with her uncle when he went to check the house.

After dark, to evade the flashing cameras, they drove back to Emma's home. Her uncle took in the mail. "Here's some for you, Emma."

She had a postcard with a dolphin on the front, and on back, a scrawled message from Revi. "Hang in there, Em; I know she's innocent. I'll be home soon."

Emily's vision blurred. Some of her high school friendships might not last through her mother's murder trial when it came, she thought. But then, the ones that turned away from her wouldn't have been much of friends to start with. She'd have Revi, and she'd have Luke on her side. There was a note from him, too, sealed. She tucked it inside her jeans pocket, to read privately later.

She climbed the stairs to her parents' room—her dad

should be allowed to leave the hospital soon—and looked through her mom's jewelry box until she found a tiny key. It fit the smallest drawer of her mother's antique desk. Emma felt like an intruder, but her mother had said to do this.

Emma turned the key and pulled open the drawer. Under some rose-colored notepaper, she saw a small notebook. It opened easily to her touch, and she flipped to one of the earlier pages and began to read.

Dear Diary:

I dreamed again last night. I felt the horror, the pain, just as if it were happening for the first time. I was there on the sidewalk, with the rest of our group clustered in a loose circle. Around me, I could hear the mob—people yelling, shouting ugly names—and I staggered from the rough shoving hands. I was being thrust away from my friends— I tried to find a familiar face, reached for a hand that I trusted, but it wasn't there.

Low and deep beneath the shouts of the crowd, I heard the K-9 dogs growl, their lips drawn back over fangs that I could already feel tearing my skin. I saw the blue uniforms, the closed faces as the police moved to push us back. Then I looked around, searching for the one face most important to me, so we could blend into the rest of the unruly mob and slip away.

But he didn't come. I stumbled through the crowd, trying to find him, glancing into the nearest building . . .

Then fire blossomed behind the glass door, and splinters of glass exploded outward, with a wave of sound that knocked me to my knees.

I felt the fear in my throat and the wetness of blood trickling down my face, and I knew something had gone terribly wrong . . .

Epilogue

Dear Diary:

I'm writing this in Mom's diary, but soon I hope I can give the book back to her. It seems like a long time ago when I went to Los Angeles to find my shadow self; I found as well a lot of truths I sometimes still wish I'd never discovered.

Luke says I will be glad to know the truth, someday, and he thinks my mom is glad, too, now that the whole thing is over, and she's almost free again. Living a lie isn't an easy thing to do. The truth will set you free, my dad says.

After months of legal wrangling, the police decided they didn't have enough evidence to try Mom as an accessory to murder (maybe because it was never true!), but they got her for evading arrest, and her lawyer arranged a plea bargain. The judge let her go on probation for time served plus six months. She missed my eighteenth birthday, and Todd's and Ethan's birthdays, and her and Dad's nineteenth anniversary, and Mother's Day, and Christmas, and a lot of ordinary things besides. But at least she'll get to see me graduate from high school, and Todd from middle school.

They're releasing her a week from Thursday; we're all counting the hours. I got my acceptance to UCLA last week, and I'm hoping to room with Sophie again, this time for real. (Revi is still set on attending Yale, but she promises to come out and visit.)

And Luke says he'll be at the airport when I arrive in the fall, with a really big balloon and a bigger kiss . . .

LIFE AT SIXTEEN

You're Not a Kid Anymore.

Being sixteen isn't easy. Whether you laugh or whether you cry, that's life.

___**LIFE AT SIXTEEN: BLUE MOON**
by Susan Kirby 0-425-15414-9/$4.50

___**LIFE AT SIXTEEN: SECOND BEST**
by Cheryl Lanham 0-425-15545-5/$4.50

___**LIFE AT SIXTEEN:**
NO GUARANTEES
by Cheryl Lanham 0-425-15974-4/$4.50

___**LIFE AT SIXTEEN:**
GOOD INTENTIONS
by Cheryl Lanham 0-425-16521-3/$4.50

___**LIFE AT SIXTEEN: SILENT TEARS**
by Cheryl Zach 0-425-16739-9/$4.50